NORTHLAND FRAIL

UNDER THE HORN OF HEARTH

S.P. ROWE

Duck 'n Row
11024 Balboa Blvd., #268, Granada Hills, CA 91344
info@ducknrow.com

Paperback ISBN: 979-8-9928411-1-4
Hardcover ISBN: 979-8-9928411-0-7
Ebook ISBN: 979-8-9928411-2-1

Front cover art by Ambient Pixel Design
Interior design by Jess LaGreca, Mayfly book design

Library of Congress Catalog Number: 2025904614
First Printing: 2025

To my wife, family, and friends, who were very patient with me as they read my drafts and listened to my nonstop stories throughout the development of this world.

CONTENTS

THE SONG OF CREATION

O nly darkness existed.

In this place of no beginning and no end, in this womb of nothingness, awakened the giant named *Rasmus*. The loneliness of the dark enveloped her, prevailing within and without. Yet in this silence, she spoke, banishing the void with the power of her voice.

She spoke of the sky, and the sky was created. She spoke of the ground, and the ground appeared. Lo', then she created *The Keepers* to watch over them: *Baldr* of the sky and *Freya* of the ground.

"This is good."

Rasmus smiled, feeling joy from her new creation. Then she explored the world for a time. Yet, soon her loneliness returned, and neither the majesty of the sky nor the comfort of the land could make it depart.

Noticing this, Freya approached Rasmus and asked, "Mother of all things, how can your emptiness be filled?"

At that moment, Rasmus describes her ideal companions—conjuring The First Ones.

They were *Vuloospa*.

They were perfect.

They wanted for nothing.

. . . and they sang unto her.

—Freya's Lamentations 1:1

CHAPTER 1

SHADOWS IN STALDEN

Clop-ity, crunch.

Clop-ity, crunch.

Boots trot and skid across gravel and stone, echoing on the mortar of an ancient parapet. For untold generations, the walls of *Stalden Keep* have stood firm and weathered, denying all enemies both brave and foolish enough to accept its challenge. A chill wind blows across its brick face, scoffing these attempts down through the ages, as ancient bones bleach in the pale moonlight of *Iz*—the giant sphere of ice bearing infinite witness from the sky. But tonight, the intruders are within.

"Rolf!" A voice whispers, "Rolf . . . stop!"

Rolf, a fair-haired boy of seventeen, emerges from the shadows with a satchel slung over his shoulder. He makes a mad dash across the dimly lit courtyard, legs pumping with mechanical precision.

Rolf has a strong and tall build; only his face gives away his youth. Pale skin glistens with sweat as he sprints toward the rampart opposite *Stalden Keep*, the hall of their forebearers. Its dark windows now glow with the flickering flame of torchlight.

"Brother, wait!"

A second, younger boy, Erlann, of fifteen spans, appears in the keep's doorway. Cut from the same cloth, Erlann lacks the benefit of his older brother's longer stride. He huffs for a moment, recapturing his breath as his eyes strain after Rolf.

1

Rolf lobs the satchel over the edge of the rampart and climbs down as Erlann reaches the edge, panting.

"Rolf, bring it back."

Erlann looks over his shoulder; the faint sound of guards stir alarms in the keep.

"We were just going to look!"

Erlann swallows hard, swinging his leg over the edge.

"It's forbidden to hold a sword!"

Rolf glances up, shooting Erlann an ornery smirk.

"I'll pass *The Trials* soon enough," Rolf scoffs. "The only thing you will ever swing is your prick!"

"Not so!" Erlann fires back.

"Come on then and prove me false!"

Erlann glances toward *Stalden Keep*, now ablaze in the red anger of torches.

"Fine, Rolf! Fine!"

He swings over the side of the wall, gingerly placing himself on the stones for support. Just then, he looks past his feet to Rolf's judgmental expression. *He's going to best me again*, Erlann thinks. Sure enough, Rolf lets go of the wall and free falls to ground level. His boots land with a mighty thud, splitting the wood of the walkway. A perfect landing.

"Hold!"

Alas, there's always a bigger boulder on the mountainside. Erlann looks toward the voice, up top. The first thing he sees is scalps on a warrior's shield, patches of hair, and rotting flesh on old, dried-out, blood-stained wood.

"Who are you, boy?! Speak!"

Erlann wonders how the guards could have reacted with such speed. He looks past the shield to the warrior himself. He's an old man with a big build and a long, braided beard. Wrinkles and deep, weather-worn skin pock his accusing face, a ferocious visage that only torchlight could exaggerate so remarkably.

"Name, boy!"

Erlann freezes; this is no mere *Brond Here* but a *First Spear* of the

Brond Voldur. Thanes of *Stalden Keep*, bled by battle and hardened by war. Handpicked by the council, they stand above petty power and faction, stewards of *The Gathering*, protectors of hearth and song.

Erlann looks away with shame in his heart. The proud warrior shifts his gaze to Rolf. Below, Rolf tries to hide the satchel; but as he does, the hilt of a sword slides out. They're caught! The sentry's scaled armor glistens as bright as the accusation in his eyes.

"Thief!" The *First Spear* roughly shouts.

"No! Wait!"

Erlann doesn't have time to finish. With contempt, the *First Spear* swings his torch at Erlann who ducks! Then, the *First Spear* draws his sword as Erlann holds up his hands in protest.

"Hold! I am—"

"Look out!" gasps Rolf.

The *First Spear* swings his sword as Erlann's feet slip to the next gap in the rocks! The blade misses him by inches, sparking against the stone of the rampart's top. Erlann wobbles against the wall for a moment but spares himself an immediate fall to the bottom, as he hears Rolf's full-throated laugh floating up from below.

"Ha! He has seen too many winters, brother!"

"And me not enough!" Erlann rasps quietly.

The *First Spear* recovers for a second swing. With a roar, he brings across a mighty blow! Catching only the rock; Erlann has swung to another stone, just in time. The sentry growls.

Rolf laughs, "Brother, get down here!"

But the *First Spear* is strong; his next blow shatters the rock that Erlann is hanging onto. Erlann drops his hand a moment before the blow lands, holding on with his remaining other hand.

"Jump!" Rolf yells.

Erlann looks behind himself, comparing his height to Rolf's level. Not a chance he can jump. The *First Spear* shakes his embedded sword, attempting to free it from the stone. Erlann pulls himself up, and as the *First Spear* struggles, he climbs up and out through the old man's legs.

"Stop playing and jump," Rolf exclaims jokingly.

Erlann bolts to the corner of the rampart wall, now ablaze with torches. Guards close in from all ends. Erlann is trapped. Rolf looks around and sees a blacksmith's tent under the rampart.

"Jump to the tent! The tent!"

Erlann eyes the guards closing in.

"Will it hold?"

Rolf hesitates.

"Will it hold?" Erlann's voice echoes on the wind.

"Yes! Now jump, fool!" Rolf retorts.

The *First Spear*, flanked now by two other guards, points toward Erlann, "I'll have your pretty locks for my shield!"

Erlann glances over his shoulder; suddenly, the fall doesn't seem so bad.

The *First Spear* bares his teeth, "No shame in death, little cur . . ."

Another guard sneaks quietly toward Erlann.

"To the 'True Death' with you!" the *First Spear* speaks with finality.

He nods to the sneaking guard—it's a signal, a quiet command to strike Erlann dead where he stands! Rolf sees the trick and calls to him.

"Erlann!"

The *First Spear* stops in his tracks.

"Erlann?"

"Jump!" Rolf waves his brother downward.

Erlann takes a deep breath and moves toward the edge.

The sneaking guard lifts his sword for the killing blow! But the *First Spear* raises his hand. The sneaking guard obeys, stopping in place. Erlann takes a deep breath and jumps, screaming as he falls down!

Rip! Erlann hits the top of the tent and tears right through the fabric, hitting the hard smithing anvil below. Rolf runs up and rummages through the mess of cloth and gear.

"*Freya's tears!*"

Rolf can't find Erlann; he continues to rummage. Erlann pops up from under the tent, wearing the cloth as an unintended shawl. He smiles, as a dazed expression soaks his face.

"I'm alright!" Erlann responds with a dopey smile.

A huge gash opens up on his forehead. Blood streams down Erlann's face as Rolf quickly grabs a handful of crumpled tent fabric. He tears it into a strip and ties the ribbon around Erlann's head.

"Foolish Erlann." Rolf says, his tone betraying the relief he feels at his brother's survival.

Quickly, placing hand to mouth, Rolf whistles loudly. A black steed charges toward them from out of the darkness; well kept and strong, he's a horse fit for a prince. Rolf helps Erlann up onto the saddle as they attempt their escape.

"Close the gate!" orders the *First Spear* from the parapet.

The sound of chains groan into motion as Rolf leaps up onto the horse. The gate is closing as he leans forward, loosening the reigns.

"Ya!"

Erlann and Rolf reach the gate just in time, passing through as it shuts. The *First Spear* pounds his hand on the rampart. He looks after Erlann and Rolf as they ride into the distance, then his eyes turn back to his fellow guards.

"Right then . . . Who wakes the *Brond Helm*?"

CHAPTER 2

THE EDGE OF THE WORLD

D awn peeks through the craggy rocks of Northland, flooding
mountain and valley alike with rich red and blue light. The two
brothers gallop away from the great hilltop city of *Alstead*, away
from duty, away from care. They pass through a menagerie of eroding
trenches, peeling pikes, and ancient engines, all slowly returning to the
dirt of *Rasmus*. A rotting record of forty thousand spans of violence waged
by cultures long ago.

Erlann steals a look back toward *Stalden Keep*, the fortress perched
atop the massive city. "Father will be furious," Erlann rasps with disappointment.

Rolf smiles. "Why would he be? His two sons only made off with his
prize sword!"

"You told me we were just going to look at the sword, Rolf!"

Rolf laughs, a full-bellied laugh. It's the laugh of a beggar who's come
upon a gold piece or a thirsty traveler who's found a lake. Somehow, this
makes Erlann even more concerned. He glares at Rolf; it's a look that only
one sibling could give to another.

"Calm yourself, Erlann! We're only borrowing it!"

Iz, the ice moon, rises behind the city of *Alstead*, which, thanks to
the two boys, has awakened much too early this day. Erlann's head rests
against his brother's back as they ride off into the dark mists of the early
morning. Erlann breathes softly as the concussion takes effect. He rolls in

and out of awareness, into a waking dream. The amount of time passing, he could not say as his mind slowly falls into darkness.

In this void, there is nothing, but somehow everything, all at once. He sees the line of his fathers from before the histories of stone, before counting, all the way back to the beginning. Then through this unknown darkness, Erlann feels a presence; he's not alone. This thing, whatever it may be, is old. Its hunger overwhelms Erlann's mind, like something blowing on dying embers of a reignited flame. Erlann breathes out carefully; a chill of great danger comes over him.

The darkness has a voice. Its speech is old, rough, and guttural.

"Seek me not, Erlann, son of Tyr. For I will hunt you . . . soon enough."

Erlann's eyes burst open with a surge of fear and dread, but he awakens once more, leaning against his brother's back as they ride down a treacherous mountain path—his teeth rattling in the freezing cold. What strange stuff the mind can conjure, thinks Erlann. *A passing dream, it must be.*

The people of Northland rarely climb this high into the mountains. There's no road through the icy north nor settlements with which to trade. Rolf, holding a look of determination, steers his horse down the ancient pathway.

"This is the trail," Rolf says with a look of recognition. "I've seen it on the stones."

"On the carvings of *Stanheng Hol!*" shudders Erlann. "What do you know of *Freya's* words? We should turn back. These heights will be the death of us both."

Erlann studies the mountainside for a moment. Carved into the crag, he sees derelict buildings and collapsing overlooks—signs of an untold labyrinth within. The stone, once beautifully crafted by the hands of the finest artisans, is now weather-worn and beaten by a cruel winter wind. It's as if, one day, this great city ended, and its host simply walked away. Even now, this ancient civilization blends masterfully into the rock, frozen in time, impossible to see but from a short distance. He's heard of these people, these *Men of the Mountains,* and their retreat from the surface for reasons unknown.

Rolf studies the landscape. "It should be just, up here."

They ride on.

Then, beyond the curve of the road, they see it. A gigantic glacier, more a fortress than of natural make. Its surface is lined with a multitude of icicles resembling a razor-boar's back, prickling into a triangular sharp spire of ice stabbing upward into the sky.

Erlann scans the glacier, it's almost as if the ice is trying to escape from the earth itself. He feels that if this frosty construct could speak, it would scream, *"Stop, turn back. Evil rests here."*

Rolf jumps off the horse, satchel in hand, stomping his way through the thick snow. Erlann dismounts and pauses a moment. He feels eyes on him. He turns and sees a cloaked figure watching from a nearby rock. The figure quickly ducks down, evading his notice.

A trick of the light? Erlann wonders. A place like this can vex the mind terribly.

Rolf turns and hollers, "Come on!"

Erlann hesitates, then follows. The pair run on, wading through a thick snow drift. Rolf turns back toward his brother, a look of amazement and discovery flashing across his face.

"There it is. Just like in song and stone." Rolf gives Erlann a look, as if testing him. "Do you know it?"

"Isen Mur," Erlann says after some hesitation.

Rolf smiles.

"This is where the Great Hunt ended. A mighty battle was fought in this place."

Erlann looks past his brother at the expansive compound. It's beautiful, dangerous, and filled with deep fissures and treacherous drop-offs. Rolf's so excited he tries to draw a breath as he exhales, coughing into the frosty wind. Erlann laughs, the boot is finally on the other foot!

"Tired, Rolf?" Erlann asks, smiling.

He pushes Rolf as he brushes past him.

"Hey!" chokes Rolf.

Erlann turns back toward Rolf to gloat and is hammered in the face with a snowball. Rolf laughs, pleased with his surprise attack. Erlann hastily packs a handful of snow and wings it toward Rolf. They both leap, and scoop, and throw as fast as possible; their laughter resounding on the mountainside.

Erlann winds up his arm, exclaiming, "For the free north!"

He throws multiple snowballs at Rolf, who bats them away.

"Arrows? Bah! A coward's weapon!" Rolf says as he thumps his chest.

Erlann jumps down the hill and slides toward a lower plateau. Rolf jumps after him, grabbing an icicle from a nearby rock. Erlann skids onto the glacier, spinning on his back as he lands. Rolf hits the ice as well— laughing as he barrel-rolls onto the ledge.

The two settle on the glacier, digging in their feet to slow their speed of pace. As he stops, Erlann finds himself at the edge of a giant drop-off. He stares into a frozen river hundreds of feet down and realizes, in that moment, that anything closer would have sent him over the edge to his death.

Rolf looks over Erlann's shoulder and whistles. "That's a long way down."

They both laugh for a moment, catching their breath. Suddenly, Rolf raises his icicle and playfully swipes at Erlann.

"Ow!" Erlann recoils from the stinging pain as he looks down at his forearm.

The icicle has torn a small hole in the skin. Crimson liquid seeps from the porous gap into the chilly air. It's so cold the wound freezes closed almost immediately. Rolf leans in with concern in his eyes.

As he does so, Erlann looks up at Rolf's satchel, eyeing the sword's hilt hanging near him. Erlann quickly pulls the sword.

Shiiiiiiiiiiiiing!

He stands in the ready position with the sword drawn. There's an undeniable tension between the two kin.

Are they brothers? Rivals? Both.

Erlann turns his glare from Rolf to the sword, admiring it from blade to grip. Though spans old, it still shines as if freshly forged. He sees the hilt made of silver metal, fit for a *Brond Helm* of the Free North indeed. Under the thick guard, carved into the pommel, is a strange symbol: a flower made of stone.

Rolf admires it. "Father's sword. *The Boon of Stor Doren.*"

He drops the icicle as Erlann studies the sword; it's intoxicating. It's not only a weapon but a symbol of leadership. From his high seat in *Stalden*

Keep, Brond Helm Tyr leads the *Brond Voldur*, the city guard, and all of the *Brond Here* in the eastern hold.

"Hard to share a sword," Rolf says with *brond* in his voice.

Before Erlann can react, Rolf pulls a trick move, getting the sword back.

Erlann is growing quite frustrated with Rolf's selfishness. "Fine, take it then!"

"I have. Haven't I?" sneers Rolf.

Erlann bites his tongue and moves toward the drop-off once again. He looks out over the high mountains and frozen river below, searching for any signs of life or kingdom.

Erlann whispers, *"The Men of the Mountains."*

"You search in vain," Rolf says flatly. "No one has seen them since their great war, not on the surface anyway. That's if grandmother didn't make them up altogether." Rolf swings the sword, dangerously close to Erlann.

"Rolf! Mind yourself!" Erlann protests.

In that moment, Erlann no longer sees his brother but the hard stare of an enemy warrior. Will it come to this in the greater span of time?

Rolf growls, "Never turn your back on my blade . . . brother or no."

Erlann doesn't know how to answer that.

"I've heard *Brond Here* say this sword can cut through anything." Rolf wonders aloud, "Should we test it?"

Erlann stands still, not wanting to provoke Rolf. Rolf brings the sword high over his head with a mighty scream! But he's not aiming for Erlann. The sword cuts into the glacier, piercing its surface.

The ice groans with a mighty howl.

Erlann jumps back! His voice stripped of the pretense of bravery.

"Rolf, did you hear that?"

Rolf lets out a hearty laugh.

"You should have seen yourself! Your face!"

Erlann has had enough.

"It's getting colder, brother. Let's go back before the light is lost."

Rolf reaches for the sword. It's stuck. He pulls harder.

Erlann cannot hide his annoyance with the situation.

"Rolf! Enough with this child's play!"

But Rolf's not joking. He struggles and strains against the ancient ice, trying to free their father's sword from its merciless grip. Then, pulling with all his might and with a sharp groan of scraping metal, he draws the sword from the ice.

Erlann rushes to his brother's side. Forgetting all else, he holds his breath in fear for the sword.

Rolf inspects the blade and remarks, "I was sure I bent it, ruined it, but see? Not a scratch!

CRACK.

Rolf freezes.

Erlann listens intensely and whispers, "What was that?"

A second CRACK, louder than before, rips past their ears.

A small split forms in the ice, an opening breaking toward Erlann.

Rolf holds out his arms and warns, "Be still."

The crack in the ice spreads toward Erlann's feet as Rolf carefully inches toward him.

The crack pulls farther apart, making a RUMBLING sound below the fissure as Rolf holds out the hilt of the sword.

"Grab on!"

Erlann reaches for the handle, but it's too far. He shifts . . . just a little closer . . .

SPLIT!

Without warning, a hole opens, but under Rolf's feet! Fear grips Rolf's face as he falls straight into the fissure.

"Rolf!!!" Erlann yells, charging for the opening.

He quickly leaps onto his knees, spreading out his weight evenly as the force of his lunge carries him to the edge. Erlann whips his head over the side of the newly formed gap. Looking down into the chasm, he sees Rolf, a few feet away, hanging by the hilt of their father's sword. Below Rolf is a mishmash of ice and rock . . . the anatomy of *Isen Mur*.

Erlann hollers, "Hold on!"

He draws a dagger from his boot and strikes the frozen ground. The blade of his knife bounces off the ice. Erlann tries again, jabbing harder! This time his knife takes, but only just a little. It will have to be enough. As Erlann holds onto his dagger with one hand, he reaches down for Rolf.

"Brother! Grab my hand!"

Erlann desperately strains to reach Rolf's arm as the dagger begins to slide. He renews his effort, stretching down even farther as his finger touches Rolf's.

The ground shakes, causing Erlann to lose his balance and fall! Just then, a hand grabs his—it's Rolf's! Rolf has caught him! Erlann dangles over the abyss, with nothing but black crags below and light sky above, Rolf grips his hand with grim determination.

His brother gets Erlann's attention. "See that ledge?"

Erlann sees something of an outcropping to his right.

Rolf motions and whispers, "One. Two . . ."

The ground shakes again. Rolf's hand begins to slip.

"Now!"

Erlann swings over to the little ledge just in time to see his brother slip and fall on top of him. With a THUD, Erlann is knocked off the ledge. Now hanging upside down, looking up, he sees Rolf holding onto his feet. Erlann notices the sword again. It has fallen to an outcrop just below.

Rolf commands, "Erlann! Swing up! Give me your hand!"

Erlann says, "Father's sword!"

He reaches for the sword, stretching his arms as far as they will go. Muscles straining, his bones almost pop out of their sockets.

"Forget it!" Rolf exclaims in desperation.

Erlann pushes as far as he can and then pushes farther as a single finger touches the hilt.

"Erlann! Let it go!"

Erlann smiles.

"I have it!"

Erlann's fingers grasp the sword.

"Erlann!" Rolf pleads.

Erlann tries to reach up for Rolf's hand, but it's no good.

Rolf can only watch helplessly as his hold slips . . .

Down.

Down.

Erlann drops with their father's sword in hand—into the deep darkness of Isen Mur.

CHAPTER 3

A PRISONER IN THE DARK

S PLASH! The unexpected warmth of a hot spring embraces Erlann's body as its waters thaw and caress him. Erlann's eyes open to bubbles everywhere . . . bubbles leading the way up. Erlann follows their instruction with intention, swimming hard, as he breaks through to the surface of a subterranean pool.

After rasping in the stale cavern air for what seems an eternity, he looks around this place where he has fallen, taking its measure. It's an ice cave, cleaner than the surface, undamaged and protected from the centuries above.

"Erlann!" Rolf's voice can be heard faintly from above.

Erlann looks up toward the voice whose terror and dismay match the size of the glacier itself. He spies a light from the fissure at the top. The opening is hopelessly high; even the daylight cannot reach him.

Erlann finds his footing and calls up toward the fissure.

"I live!" Erlann yells.

Rolf answers, "Stay there. I will find a way down!"

Erlann takes a moment to gather his strength, and then pulls himself out of the pool with Tyr's sword in hand. It's dark in the cavern, and Erlann shivers, adjusting his eyes to the pitch.

The surrounding area looks like the inside of an old structure, yet the purpose of this derelict construct is lost to the stones—having been almost entirely covered by countless spans of crawling ice. Erlann spies some dead roots embedded in the frosty cobblestones and brushes them out of the way. Below the roots, he spies a grayish-green stone embedded in the earth.

Erlann smiles, thinking, *Some good fortune at last.*

"The stone that burns!" he exclaims.

Ripping out the roots, Erlann makes a modest pile of kindling at the pool's edge. Then he strikes the grayish-green stone against his father's sword. Nothing yet. He stops for a moment and blows into his hands to warm them, and then strikes the stone again.

A spark!

Erlann breathes a deep sigh of appreciation. The fire crackles and pops, sputtering to life.

"Stay strong, little fire."

As Erlann warms himself, here, at the bottom of the world; the fire sparks upward, escaping to where he cannot follow. Then, Erlann hears something. It comes softly at first—a quiet laugh, a woman's laugh.

"What trickery is this?" Erlann mutters to himself as he lifts Tyr's sword, listening. "Who's there?"

Another female laugh, from behind him this time. He's being circled—a hunter's tactic.

Erlann turns!

He sees no one, only darkness yet again. Erlann grabs a root from the fire and points his makeshift torch toward the laughter. He sees several holes in the ice that "honeycomb" their way throughout the chamber. From deep inside one of these holes, something watches him.

It's in the shape of a woman. Her skin shines pale in the firelight, like cold porcelain. Her hair is sharp and frozen, the product of 100,000 spans in the northern chill.

She's watching. Stalking.

Erlann immediately lifts the sword, unsure what he's seeing. He tracks her with its point, awaiting the first move.

Suddenly, a second entity speaks from across the cavern. This husky voice pierces Erlann to the bone. He recognizes it immediately as the voice from his dream.

"Teeth so big . . . for a pup so small . . ."

A low, piercing growl fills the cavern.

"Have you come to face the beast?!"

The cavern shakes, almost as if in fear of the voice's power.

"No. Yours is a different purpose."

Erlann hears the rattle of chains dragging across the stone and ice as something moves toward him from the dark. He strains his eyes as he holds his torch closer, making out a gigantic silhouette against the firelight.

Erlann shudders at a thought he has not yet considered.

"Are you the spirit of *Baldr* come to take me to his halls?" hazards Erlann.

"No."

After a long silence, Erlann tries again. "I'm not dead?"

"Not yet."

It's coming closer. Something big. Erlann spies two fiery reddish-yellow eyes opening; they float toward him, cutting through the dark. The porcelain woman sings; this is answered by another more distant female voice . . . and then another . . . and another. Erlann listens to the disquieting sounds.

The male voice speaks again, "They sing with a hate from the dawning of creation. Of a paradise lost to them forever."

Erlann looks at the pale and leathery-looking woman. She hasn't moved. She still stands in the same spot, but continues singing softly from the hole in the chamber wall.

Erlann desperately wants to understand her. He asks, "Is she a spirit?"

"She is First Born."

"First Born?" echoes Erlann.

The guttural voice continues, "The *Vuloospa*—once perfected in form and spirit by the maker's hand are now ruined and accursed; almost extinguished by *the Men of The Mountains*. They persist in this place, where not even *Stor Doren* will venture."

The *Vuloospa* snarls, her lips curl upright into a grotesque sneer, revealing razor sharp teeth. Erlann looks on with equal parts revulsion and fascination. Above all, he dares not look away.

"Is she an animal or man?"

"Put away your sword, man-pup."

Erlann lowers the weapon. Sensing an opening, the *Vuloospa* in the hole inches toward him, apparently with her appetite growing. Without warning, a bestial roar rattles the chamber. Overwhelmed, the *Vuloospa* stops in her tracks. Looking past Erlann, she turns and scurries back into the hole.

Erlann balks, while exclaiming, "She's gone? Why?"

"She fears more than she hungers . . . for now."

Erlann knows if the *Vuloospa* are afraid, it's not of him. He peers into the dark, pondering the nature of this thing that restrains them. Feeling a little braver, Erlann inches closer to the voice. With his makeshift torch and sword in hand, he hears his feet crunching against the cold floor as the voice speaks again.

"Brave boy. Come closer."

"My prison is a monument to the frailty of men."

Erlann's small fire has been going for some time. As the kindling burns down, he notices the ice on the wall is rapidly melting. Water runs down in a small flood as the stability of the ice fractures.

CRACK. Something breaks loose from the ice. Erlann looks and sees a skeleton wielding a mace coming out of the wall toward him!

"*Freya's tears!*" Erlann screams in terror.

But this is no magic—just the weight of ages, as the lifeless skeleton collapses at Erlann's feet. Erlann looks around the cold chamber. It's quite the menagerie of fallen dead. They are rich and poor, Eastmen and Westmen—refugees, as well, from the burning south. Their many skeletons line the walls and floor, being slowly metabolized by the crawling ice of the pit.

The voice from the pitch speaks again.

"Does anyone remember him, do you think?" Erlann marks the dead warrior at his feet, as the voice continues, "Was he loved? Or hated? In some distant part of the world, do they still sing songs to honor his name? Or does he lie cold and forgotten, a victim of his own hollow ambition?"

Erlann looks at his feet. He sees that bodies are all around him now. Vaulting from side to side, he tries to avoid stepping on the corpses, but each sickening crunch of his boots mock the attempt. Erlann, at first afraid, calms himself and looks at the fallen skeleton's hand. The mace now rests apart from it having rolled across the floor. With the utmost respect and compassion, Erlann reaches down and places the mace back in the skeleton's grasp, crossing its arms. Erlann speaks for the dead in quiet prayer as he searches his mind for the correct words. He asks that this warrior, whoever he was, may enter the halls of Baldr, where one may live forever.

Then, the voice gloats in the dark saying, "You speak to ears that can no longer hear; his gods are long dead. You know not his prayers, Erlann."

Erlann freezes and wonders, *How does he know my name?*

"Am I known to you?" Erlann asks. He hears a sniffing sound from the shadows.

"I smell your hunger and know it well, Erlann. It burns in all the people of Rasmus. Answer this well or die this day."

The voice speaks again,

"In the grand arena where powers collide,
Chained and yearning, I bide my time.
My hunger's sharp, my teeth laid bare,
Ambition's thirst draws them unaware.
When bonds are shattered, my fate unfurls,
I'll rise at last to consume the world."
"What am I?"

Erlann thinks for a moment and wonders if the future is so bleak.

"You are the end of all Rasmus. The twilight of time itself."

Erlann's answer is met with stone quiet.

He breaks the silence and demands, "Show yourself."

A huge wolf's head emerges from the shadows and into the firelight. Old runes are carved into its fur from a purpose and time long forgotten. Its mane, though once lovingly cared for it seems, is now old and overgrown with braids split and falling out. The canine's lips curl into a haunting smirk. Around its neck hangs a huge steel collar with multiple chains fixed to the wall.

"Correct."

Erlann's blood runs cold as the beast closes in. The chains rattle and bounce, revealing a large amount of slack. The monster could have lunged upon him at any moment, swallowing him whole. Erlann runs out of room to retreat, bracing his back against the chamber wall.

"I am Fenreir. Look into my eyes, young warrior, and know your future."

Erlann snarls and taunts him, "Come then, monster, I am not afraid."

Fenreir lowers his mighty head with a quiet laugh, his massive form pressing closer. Erlann sees the beast shudder with a tremor that speaks of excitement barely restrained. The wolf's presence is overwhelming, his hunger palpable, a craving long denied—and now teetering on the edge of release.

Erlann wastes no more time and looks into the wolf's eyes. He sees his own reflection haunting him from the darkness. As he leans in further, making eye contact with himself, Erlann drowns in the black pitch of Fenreir's pupil. He's lost all sense of time and place. It's dark, wet, he's swimming now, Erlann surfaces, gasping for air. It's a race of some kind; he's pushing himself to pass the other boys. He scoops a handful of water, but instead of a lake, he pushes himself to the top of a mountain, climbing cliffs! He hears an animal cry, its echo resounding in the distance. The scream sounds almost human now as a warrior takes a swing for his head. Erlann ducks, bringing his hand to his own face. He spies blood on his fingers. He's lost his left eye! He's much older now, middle-aged, fighting foes. Erlann kicks out the leg of his attacker, felling him to the ground. He stretches back his sword arm, preparing to strike his brother who has fallen onto his back. Rolf lets out a horrified gasp as Erlann stabs downward toward his face. But instead of an impact, his hand lands on the arm of a chair; not just any chair but a throne. The throne of Northland. Grey hairs adorn Erlann's scalp as he gazes out of his remaining good eye. It's a magnificent feast. Erlann presides over the funeral pyre of his brother Rolf, raising his cup to the cheers of adoring warriors. He wears the crown, a king of Northland.

Erlann looks on, horrified, and gasps, "No!"

From the dark, Fenreir's jaws open, consuming the king, himself.

"No!" Erlann breaks eye contact with the wolf and dodges out of the way. *What lies and sorcery is this?* he wonders.

"You are mistaken, monster. The men of the Free North rule themselves."

Fenreir howls as the chamber shakes.

Taking the opportunity to move away from the wall, Erlann lifts his father's sword.

Erlann's voice cuts with hostility, "Careful, monster. Though I am small, I will not go easily."

The *Vuloospa* fill the chamber in great numbers as Fenreir extends to his full height, once again.

"Remember this, man-pup: in the dawn of your life, it's not the howl of the wolf, but the growl of the bear you must fear."

Erlann's eyes fill with confusion, as he asks, "What are you?"

"I was the destroyer of paradise. Betrayer of my master. Eater of the world. I am the end of your story and all stories to come."

Erlann lowers his sword, considering Fenreir's words.

This is the opening the *Vuloospa* have been waiting for. Suddenly, they charge into the chamber . . . dozens of them.

Fenreir sneers, "Man-pup! Guard yourself!"

The *Vuloospa* hiss, raising their arms to attack! Their boney fingers, ground into sharp and skinless claws, rake for Erlann's body.

Erlann counter-strikes with his father's sword as the *Vuloospa* lunge away with amazing agility.

Erlann turns as three more emerge, ready to make the kill.

Fenreir stomps his foot as the cavern shakes with his intense, long growl.

The *Vuloospa* stop and cower.

Fenreir roars, "Þetta *kjöt er mitt!*"

They back away as Fenreir stretches to his true height. He's gigantic . . . filling the cavern.

"Now, go, man-pup!"

Erlann looks past the *Vuloospa*, toward the hot pool in the center of the room.

"The water here is swift. It will lift you up," instructs Fenreir.

Erlann looks to the water and then back at Fenreir.

"You have my thanks, monster," Erlann replies.

Fenreir smiles and warns him, "We will meet again, King Erlann . . . Now go!"

One *Vuloospa* cannot hold her appetite back anymore and charges for Erlann! In a blink, Fenreir snatches her up into his jaws. Erlann, gripping his father's sword tightly, plunges back into the warm water. The last thing Erlann sees before he breaks the surface is Fenreir, shaking the *Vuloospa* apart, crushing and ripping her carcass in his powerful jaws.

Peering through bubbles, Erlann sees a tunnel carved through the rocks at the bottom of the pool. He paddles hard with the current as Fenreir stomps his foot into the water.

Looking behind him, Erlann sees a tide of current rushing toward him.

Erlann screams out the remaining air from his lungs as he shoots through the tunnel.

Up! Up! Up!

He's running out of breath, where this tunnel ends he knows not.

On the surface, Rolf hears a rumble. He lowers himself, listening to the rising sound of water. Trying to locate the source of this earthquake, he puts his ear to the ground. Suddenly, Erlann flies up out of a hot geyser, right in front of Rolf!

"Yaaaaaa!" Erlann yelps while doing somersaults through the air.

Rolf laughs as he pulls Erlann from the water.

"You have taken a good bath!"

Erlann spits water and then looks at his brother with pure bewilderment.

"I live? I live!"

Rolf bursts into laughter as Erlann joins in. Then a look of horror washes over Erlann's face as he remembers:

"Father's sword!"

Erlann searches around in the snow for a moment.

"Brother," warns Rolf.

Erlann looks across to the other side of the hot pool as a rough hand retrieves Tyr's sword. Several men stare at the brothers from across the water, their eyes wary, seeing through Rolf and Erlann as though they have kept watch for a thousand spans. Clothed in fur with distinct purple cloaks adorned with the emblem of *Stor Doren*—the captain stands in the center, inspecting their father's sword which bears the same mark.

The Men of the Mountains . . .

Erlann thinks as he moves toward the mountaineers.

Rolf hazards to speak, "Careful, brother."

Erlann walks up, shivering, as Rolf continues, "I've heard they sometimes take folk who wander the high roads, those travelers are never seen again."

The burly leader of the mountaineers studies Erlann as he approaches, watching for any false move. Erlann searches for words, but the captain of the mountain men sounds out a question first. Not in Storn Gar, the fabled language of the mountains, but in the tongue of the surface.

"Y-o-u-r-s?"

"It belongs to our father," Erlann answers carefully.

The mountaineer considers, partially unsheathing the blade.

Rolf reacts in protest, "Erlann!"

Erlann holds out his hand, as if to say, Rolf wait, it's alright. The captain examines the sword for a moment, smiles, and sheaths it back into the scabbard.

"*Stor Doren* sword. Good."

The captain holds out the weapon, its hilt facing Erlann. Taking the sword, Erlann embraces it to his chest, nodding toward the captain with respect.

"And it was so." Erlann gestures his thanks.

Rolf sighs in relief.

The captain turns his ear to listen. They can all hear it now, rising shrieks coming up from the mouth of an ice cave with a thunderous gallop—the nightmarish scream of the *Vuloospa*.

The Men of the Mountains draw their weapons and dash for the cave opening as a group of *Vuloospa* emerge from the mouth of the cave, howling their hate. The leading *Vuloospa* leaps high into the air . . . CRACK! She's hit by the captain's hammer, knocking her backward. Quickly the mountaineers fall into line, with hammer and shield, a wall is swiftly formed. Carefully, *the Men of the Mountains* push the *Vuloospa* back into the cave.

Rolf looks on, eyes big as saucers, witnessing the battle. "Well, alright then!" Rolf leans forward to join the fray, but Erlann swiftly grabs his shoulder.

"Rolf! We must go."

"And miss a good fight?" Rolf retorts!

Erlann points to the sword. "Shall we fall down another hole and see what comes?"

Rolf pauses, knowing Erlann is right. "You bore me, brother." Rolf shrugs. "Enough of this!"

The boys quickly mount their steed and ride away. As they speed apace, Erlann glances back toward the mouth of the cave. The armored shield wall of the mountaineers has almost pushed the last of the *Vuloospa* back into the darkness. Then suddenly, in one final bid for freedom, the lead *Vuloospa* leaps on top of their shields. She stares at Erlann and then claws at the sky, with equal parts fury and despair as she's carried back into the darkness.

Rolf laments, "If we don't hurry back, Father's going to kill you!"

"Me?!" Erlann scoffs.

He watches the glacier fade from view. Could this monster be right? Could the end of all things be nigh? One thing is certain. For this monster to succeed, Erlann knows he must be king. He will reject the crown at all costs, simple enough. The monster's words haunt his ears, like a hot brand permanently on his mind:

"I am the end of this story and all stories to come . . ."

Erlann meditates on this for a moment, "My tale will end with your death, monster . . ."

"This is my prophecy."

CHAPTER 4

THE MAN WHO WOULD BE KING

S now falls, as the captain of the mountaineers emerges from the mouth of the cave. Stepping into the sun, he inhales deeply, slowing his breath as the fatigue of battle slowly melts into calm readiness once again. Looking up, he takes in the sharp endlessness of the cold dusk sky.

Wardens.

Jailers.

The Men of the Mountains have returned from their fight with the *Vuloospa*, trickling out from the dark mouth of the cavern. Some lean against the rocks, exhausted, while others sit, looking toward the gathering storm clouds on the horizon. Through a flurry of snow, a figure emerges. He's a hulk of a man in his forties with a shaven head. Dressed in a combination of animal skin and dark mail, his ferocious appearance matches the controlled anger in his dark eyes. He stands there for a moment with a giant war-hammer resting on his shoulder. He's Thane.

"Half-men!" Thane looks over his shoulder, confirming the approaching snowstorm at his back . . . it's an advantage he'll make good use of. The mountaineers draw their swords against Thane, who walks toward them.

"H-o-l-d!" commands the captain.

Yet, Thane does not stop. A snowstorm brews behind him in the shape of an angry cloud. To the horror of the mountaineers, the strong wind envelops Thane as he charges toward them. Whiteout. Panic sets in as the mountaineers begin to die. Thane slips in and out of visibility as he smashes each one in turn with his hammer.

It's quiet again as the wind dies down. The captain finds himself alone in the snowfall. No more screams fill his ears, only the horrible silence of death. The captain calms himself. It's time to return to the bosom of *Rasmus*. He lowers his head and speaks in Storn Gar, the language of the Mountain:

"*Fer stune assay aye, er stune aye stern.*"

Suddenly, a giant hand shoves the captain against the ice wall. Thane's face emerges through the falling snow to confront him.

Thane smirks. "You have tried to hide him from me, lo' . . . you have failed."

Thane chokes the life out of the captain with one hand. A large man, completely overpowered by Thane's size and strength.

Thane announces, "This day, my ascension begins."

The storm lifts, revealing a brutal massacre. The mountain guards have been scattered from their battle circle, now lying cold and still. Thane whistles with two large fingers as his followers emerge from the snowfall. These are Thane's warrior elite, the *Stafntaki*, dressed in wolf skin. They growl and snarl at the enemy dead as Thane looks on, smiling like a proud father.

"To your king!" he orders in a loud voice.

The *Stafntaki* cheer as Thane charges toward the mouth of the cave, tracking a bloody trail of footprints in his wake.

Thane and his men run down into the depths of the frosty corridor as several pockets of *Vuloospa* sulk in the shadows, too afraid to engage. Shortly, Thane emerges from the darkness into a great chamber of ice with a subterranean pool at the end.

Sniff. Sniff.

Fenreir notices this new intrusion and growls with his nostrils flaring. Standing in silence, Thane raises his war-hammer as his warriors draw their swords and attack! His *Stafntaki* snarl and charge, leaping through the air.

Fenreir smirks as he snatches the first warrior in his jaws, impaling him with his teeth. His massive paws slam down on several more of the advancing *Stafntaki*, maiming or killing them in droves. Yet, Thane knew this would happen, he's patient. He fades into the shadows and climbs up a wall, sneaking around to the side while the monster's attention is drawn by his warriors. Suddenly, Thane jumps from the wall onto Fenreir's head, dagger drawn. Fenreir thrashes about, trying to throw him off.

"Your power is mine!" Thane chops down on the wolf's ear, severing part of it.

As the blood sprays, Thane shouts orders, "Catch it! Catch it all!"

His warriors rush in, some with hands cupped, others hold animal skin satchels. They try to catch the blood in an orgy of spray.

Fenreir yelps and bucks Thane, who falls to the floor of the cave. Shaking off the violent impact, Thane rises to his knees. He looks up and sees Fenreir opening his jaws in anger.

Thane braces himself for the bite to come.

Chomp!

The sound of large jaws snapping shut lashes throughout the cavern. Lo', Thane slowly opens his eyes. Somehow, he still lives. His gaze meets Fenreir's who studies him for a moment, seemingly recognizing him. A smile emerges from the grotesque lips of the wolf as the mashed gore of his previous kills drip down sharp ivory fangs. Fenreir laughs, a light chuckle, as he sinks backward—disappearing into the shadows.

CHAPTER 5

UNDER A DARKENED SKY

The early morning light pours into Tyr's chamber, nestled in the heart of *Stalden Keep*. Tyr's armor, adorned with scale metal, hangs ceremoniously on the wall, illuminated by the quiet dance of torchlight.

Erlann glances guiltily at Rolf, who signals him to proceed. Carefully, Erlann places the sword on the mantle. A sigh escapes his lips as the weight of the situation resolves itself. The sword is safe now, and perhaps their identity as the burglars is still unknown? Rolf smiles, nodding toward Erlann.

Erlann, staring at the blade, is immediately filled with remorse. It's forbidden for the uninitiated to carry a sword. They may have managed to escape the consequences of their actions as they live, yet in death, will Baldr's spirit know of this act?

"Fenreir? Why do you speak of this?" Elda's old wrinkled hands dip into the cool cleansing water of the *Grenileir*.

This great river flows past the mighty city of *Alstead*, bringing trade and travelers from far and wide. Their boats and rafts, both large and small, sail by regularly, bringing goods from the far east and burning south alike.

Erlann attempts to feign a bookish curiosity rather than reveal his knowledge comes from firsthand experience.

"I have heard his mention in the songs, Grandmother, about the heroes of old."

Elda questions, "That's a tale of great sorrow. Why would you wish to hear a story that ends in tears?" Her insightful gaze fixes on Erlann.

Erlann looks up at Elda, a woman in her seventies with a gentle yet persuasive demeanor. Her piercing icy-blue eyes are a window into a ferocious intelligence that seems to know much, yet much of this lore remains hidden to Erlann who can only piece together fragments from Elda's mind, a vault rich with secrets.

Elda removes the makeshift bandage from Erlann's head, the one Rolf had hastily tied for him earlier in the day. The wound, once raw and open, now bears the early signs of infection. The edges are swollen and tinged with an angry red, radiating heat. A faint sheen of yellow-green pus pools at the surface. Erlann winces as Elda checks the skin around the wound. It feels taut and tender to the touch.

Elda nods and begins, "In the first times, the world was almost consumed by the wolf, Fenreir."

Elda reaches deep into the riverbed, pulling up a handful of clay. She narrates as she works with the muck, mashing it repeatedly with her hands.

"With every creature it ate, its hunger became more ravenous . . ."

Erlann watches as Elda shapes the clay.

She continues, "Devouring all that the giant *Rasmus* had created."

"A great hunt was assembled . . . the armies of *Stor Doren*, led by the titan *Baldr*, fought Fenreir, his former companion, in the deep dark of the frozen north! Though valiant, lo', did our savior *Baldr* fall, and all that was bright and good in the world seemed lost."

Erlann holds still as Elda applies the clay to his wound. He notices drops of his own blood disturbing his reflection in the river.

"But it was from the tears of *Baldr's* sister *Freya* . . . that *Isen Mur*, a prison of ice was formed, trapping Fenreir and his hunger. To this day, from that frozen place—our river flows. In this churning of love and sorrow the first of our kind was born."

Elda removes her hand, revealing Erlann's reflection in the water. To his shock, the wound is gone. He checks his forehead in disbelief, clearing away the pus and mud, yet no scab nor scar remains. His skin looks as shiny and new as the day of his birth.

As Erlann and Elda walk up from the riverbank, they observe Rolf sparring with another boy among the cattails. The boys clash with sticks in the manner of swordplay as they practice their skills. Completing the present exchange, they reset their stances and crack sticks again.

"Again, boy!" Rolf instructs.

The red-haired pilgrim hesitates, noticing Elda and Erlann walking toward them.

Rolf gloats, "Is that your best, traveler? Turn back! You'll win no trials here, Red!"

Rolf swings with an overconfidence that's well-known to Erlann, who observes quietly. But then, the red-haired warrior easily deflects this clumsy attack, sneaking in an elbow that bashes Rolf's nose. Rolf reaches for his face as blood begins to flow.

The red-haired traveler smirks. "I bring the Red, indeed."

Erlann laughs as the redhead grandly bows to this audience of three. Rolf, nursing his bloody nose, shoots Erlann an angry look, "Funny is it?"

Erlann suppresses his smile as Rolf turns back to the red-haired pilgrim.

Suddenly, a chill wind draws Erlann's attention. He feels danger in the air, anger on the water. Erlann realizes he's hearing the individual beat of a bird's wings and the splash of every droplet of water falling from an oar of a passing ship. What this magic is, Erlann knows not.

Time's current flows slowly all around him, a moment between moments, like a whisper between words. The others hold their places around Erlann with no awareness that he can detect. Erlann cannot move either, yet his consciousness is drawn to the river. In its sparkling reflection, Erlann witnesses the fight continuing. Suddenly, the red-haired pilgrim pulls a dagger from his sleeve and stabs Rolf in the stomach. Red turns upward toward Erlann from the water, a smile curling on his lips.

Erlann quickly breaks from this state, shaking his head. He turns back toward the two boys. Rolf is unhurt; the attack hasn't happened yet. Is this the future?

Erlann calls out, "Rolf! Knife!"

As if on cue, the red-haired pilgrim pulls a hidden dagger from his sleeve and stabs toward Rolf's stomach. Rolf reacts quickly to Erlann's warning, however, and jams the inside of Red's elbow, stopping him cold. Elda turns and scrutinizes Erlann's face; he heralded the danger before it could be known.

Rolf smirks at Red, "Sneaky boy!"

Red cackles in his face, "Cheats! Both of you!!!"

Rolf smiles and kicks him in the crotch. He stands over Red, hitting and beating the red-haired pilgrim.

"Give up?!"

Erlann winces; this is getting deadly. Elda walks up to the two, gathering her strength. She drags Rolf off Red, landing on his back, he looks up at her with bewilderment.

"Grandmother! I was winning!"

Elda whispers back, "Tell me, Rolf, what have you won?"

Rolf ponders a moment. Then, with cool self-assurance, he says, "More scars to wear proudly in battle."

Elda stares at him blankly. Rolf fires her a thousand-sun smile and staggers over to the river to wash up. Elda looks at Red for a moment as he puts himself back together.

"You have a familiar look, boy."

Erlann holds out a waterskin canteen for Red to drink. The boy is covered in dust. It looks like he's been on the road for some time.

"Hold . . ." Red lights up. "I recognize all of you. You are sons of the *Brond Helm*?"

"I wish to become a *Brond Here* as well. The *Stafntaki* tried to stamp out my desire for freedom, but I escaped their howling pits! I wish to own land, have my say, and ride with the wind in my hair!"

Rolf splashes water on his face and turns, speaking with a tone of encouragement once again, "Well, come on then. Face *The Trials* with us! First a sword, then liberty shall be forever yours."

"You have my thanks." Red beams. "I'll be no man's slave ever again!"

Rolf ushers Red toward Alstead as the two boys start down the road, swapping stories and ambitions. Left alone, Erlann watches after them, feeling like a discarded old plaything. With a slight sigh, he begins to follow them on the path as Elda quietly intercepts him. Her face is wracked with a stern expression, it's a look that Erlann has never seen before. Her eyes are darkly inquisitive.

"Erlann, how did you spot that boy's blade?"

Erlann lies, "I saw the glint of the dagger as he pulled it."

He knows immediately that Elda doesn't believe him. He reacted before there was anything upon which to react, as if he was prophesying the future itself. Could she have seen him staring into the lake? Where the others had not?

Elda nods and allows him to pass. As Erlann jogs after the two boys, he feels a hard stare fixed on the back of his head. He turns and sees Elda standing by the river, studying him.

The city of *Alstead* shines during the day. Even through the winter weather, merchants come from far and wide to ply their trade—their wares reflecting in the sun. Erlann and company walk through the main gate onto a ridge which gradually slopes upward in a ramp-like fashion around the base of the hill city. Massive walls rise alongside the path, and beyond the gatehouse, the route ascends in a concentric circle, lined with all manner of buildings at its edge. At the very top, *Stalden Keep* dominates the high ground. Its ancient walls mark a considerable contrast to the newer city that has grown under its silent watch.

As the boys approach, they look skyward toward *Rasmus*'s twin moons. It's a magnificent event, the giant glaciers of cold *Iz* being slowly eclipsed by Brond, the fire moon, its molten rings giving the impression of a dark red eye.

Erlann marvels, "Look! The eclipse."

"It's starting!" Rolf howls, giving his best impression of a wolf.

"Awwwwww Woooooooooo!"

Rolf laughs as Erlann looks above to the main gate of *Stalden Keep* and sees his father, Tyr, on the rampart. The essence of a war-chief, Tyr is a huge man with a bulky build and many scars. He towers over even the larger warriors as he looks down on preparations for the coming trials, that thing the Northlanders call *The Gathering*. As Rolf waves a joyous greeting to Tyr, Erlann realizes his brother is testing the waters, measuring their father's mood. Yet, Tyr glares ahead, ignoring them both as his anger builds.

"Greetings, Father!" Rolf yells with a smile on his face.

"He knows," warns Erlann.

"He's too busy with preparations for *The Gathering*. Calm yourself, Erlann."

Then, from behind Tyr, steps the *First Spear* onto the parapet. He stares down at the boys as he folds his arms with smug contempt.

Erlann recoils as Rolf is shaken violently by calloused hands. The *Brond Helm* Tyr tracks his son through a face that has seen many brutal campaigns, the eyes of a killer, minding Rolf with his remaining good eye. In the city of *Alstead*, the High Keeper of the Law holds office, but it's *Baldr's* laws that command authority. All *Brond Here* of the Free North understand that true order comes not from wielding power but from upholding the laws that govern all. They know the sacred stones bind everyone equally, and rebellious sons are no exception. Their father's chamber, once a place of refuge, offers no safety today.

"Again!?" Tyr rages as the fire in his hearth roars!

Rolf returns his gaze with quiet confidence.

Though Rolf's height is roughly the same as his father's, Tyr outweighs him with considerably more muscle. He's a hulk of a man with strength unmatched.

Erlann notices the *First Spear* standing next to Tyr. He watches Rolf with a smug expression as Rolf shoots an angry look back in his direction. Tyr sees this as well, locking eyes with his defiant boy.

"If you were not my son, I would hang you from the parapet."

Erlann looks on with concern; his father is as serious as an early frost on the harvest. Rolf returns Tyr's stare unflinchingly; if he's afraid of their father, he's most adept at hiding it.

There's a knock at the entrance, followed by an uncomfortable silence. Erlann, trying to be invisible, watches on; neither Rolf nor Tyr wish to break eye contact.

A second knock prevails upon them.

"*Baldr*'s wounds! Enter!" snaps Tyr.

The craftsfolk have arrived, their eyes apologetic for the interruption.

"Apologies, makers, come in," says Tyr as he dismisses the First Spear, who promptly exits.

An older craftsman pulls the cover from an easel in the center of the room. It's an unfinished family portrait: a beautiful mosaic of eggshells, glued into an assembly, then painted in a vibrant color.

Tyr returns his focus to Rolf, "*The Gathering* begins tonight."

"I will win ten swords, Father, to honor your name!" answers Rolf.

"Boy, by my name, I bind you to this house," Tyr says grimly. "Here you shall remain through *The Trials*."

Erlann gasps. Rolf clenches his fists.

"Father! You shame me!"

Tyr softens. "Come the next *gathering*, we will speak on this again."

Rolf loses his composure, and growls, "Ten spans from now?!!!"

Erlann puts his hand on Rolf's shoulder to calm him, but it does no good. Rolf swells with pride as he shrugs off his brother's touch and then storms out of the chamber. Left alone with his father, Erlann moves forward carefully, as if attempting to tame a lion.

Tyr preempts Erlann before he can speak. "Timidity, boy, is the companion of shame."

Erlann knows he'll need to find his words well. "Father. We seek only the chance to stand with our kin in *The Gathering* and earn our swords."

Tyr scans him for sincerity. The honest intensity in Erlann's eyes reassures him as he sinks back into his chair.

"Erlann, one day, I will join your mother in the Halls of *Iz*: My deeds will become a song. My body will become ash. What will they sing of you and your brother? An epic of glory or a lament of hate?"

Erlann remains silent.

Tyr explains, "Some would cheer on your brother's exploits; it took great skill to evade our guards and escape this fortress. But skill without honor is of no use to the *Brond*."

Erlann nods, the matter is resolved now. He knows better than to press Rolf's interests any further. Erlann stands by his father as the wood in the hearth pops and sizzles. The red sparks live a very short and dramatic life, dancing brilliantly in the fire until their time expires on a pile of black cinders.

CHAPTER 6

THE HORN OF HEARTH

A large horn bellows from the towers of *Stalden Keep*. The Caller, or so he's known to the *Brond* of The Free North, is an old man, warm in appearance. He holds the horn with much reverence as he performs his role.

Erlann spies the horn from a safe distance, another artifact from a time when *The Men of the Mountains* walked the surface. Made from the same material as Tyr's sword, this *Horn of Hearth*'s construction is beautiful and intricate, with many overlapping tubes. He has been told that the chambers amplify the breath that is blown, reaching every ear in Northland.

The terrain shakes as the horn calls out to Northland, with little effort on the part of The Caller.

"*The Gathering* has begun!" The *First Spear's* voice reverberates down the hall with great force and authority. He cracks open a thick oak door; within is an old storage room lined from the ceiling to floor with strong wooden chests. The *First Spear* laughs with excitement, "Alright boys, give 'em up!"

Erlann sees the guards of the *Brond Voldur* emerge from their posts throughout the keep. One by one, they draw their swords and surrender them to The *First Spear* and his aides, who place them in the chests.

The doors of the mead hall open to an indulgent spread of food and drink, which sit on long tables of cloth and wood. *The Gathering* has begun. The Brond Helm have come from every corner of Northland to speak for the stones and bear justice. Where once the people of Northland were slaves to the violent coercion of subject authority, these peacekeepers, these judges of the law, now settle disputes and strife by the word of *Baldr* himself. His words come down to them by the stones of *Freya*, keeper of the earth, that which was written in the dawning at the beginning of time. Let *Baldr*'s justice cut through darkness, both petty and grand, and shine upon all the people of the *Grenileir*—from *Stalden Keep*, to all the seven corners of the Free North beyond. Let the *Cairn Moot* commence:

The first *Brond Helm* to enter from his long journey is Nils. He's a seafaring warrior by appearance and salty as the ocean. He draws his sword, and with some separation angst, places it into the first locking mechanism of several which form a stone circle in the floor at the center of the room. The lock turns slowly, sealing in the blade of the sword. Nils sighs. Not even *Baldr* himself could pull his sword free. *Brond Helm* Erik, a dashing man of thirty-six, emerges next. With a look of pride, he locks in his sword. The shrewd *Brond Helm* Halmar follows, with others in his wake. The *Brond Helm* all place their swords in the remaining locks. Tyr enters last. He draws his sword as the host of assembled *Brond Helm* admire its craftsmanship, the boon of *Stor Doren*. He quietly places his prize into the next lock as the others have done. From his chamber balcony, overlooking the hall, Erlann watches with anticipation as the stone lock closes around his father's sword.

Atop Erlann's perch, he observes a map of Northland carved into the stone floor of the hall, revealing a sword for each of the seven corners of the north and it's Brond Helm's region of responsibility. Yet, two locks remain open, their swords yet to be placed.

"*Brond Helm*, have you steered a life worthy of *Baldr's* eyes?" The five *Brond Helm* present turn to the sound of Elda's voice.

They all begin to bow to her. She waves them off.

"My friends, let us join our voices in gathering."

Two cups crash together as laughter echoes into the rafters. The meade hall is a marvel of Northland: beautiful wood carved columns arch skyward, supported by seven stone bases. In the pillars are seven tall chairs facing each other in a circle, with many other smaller chairs and tables mixed about.

The Cairn Moot is in full swing as those of the assembly feast and have words with the Brond. *Brond Helm* Halmar sits in his tall chair as he listens to the complaints of several farmers alongside him.

One farmer states in a lordly tone, "That span of land has been in my family for nine generations. It's my land!"

"No! Tis lies, *Brond Helm*! All lies," another farmer retorts.

"You two! You make my ears bleed," complains Halmar.

Across the way from Halmar sits Tyr who milks his drink. He quietly observes the others telling stories and settling disputes. From above, Erlann looks across to Erik, who's in the middle of an elaborate tale.

"So there I was, hanging by its tail; my men, hopping around, trying to avoid the flames!"

There's a thunderous laugh as *Brond Helm* Erik bonds with the crowd.

". . . then I said, 'Get behind it!'" Erik hits them with the punchline, "'No, not in there! Don't go in there, boys!'"

The warriors laugh heartily as Tyr forces a brief smile. Returning to his cup, he notices it's empty.

Just then, a boy of sixteen enters the hall. He gazes around the room, searching the crowd for someone familiar.

Erik notices the boy and waves him over. "Ah Sven! Come in, son!"

The room grows silent; there's a quiet intensity gripping the crowd, in expectation of a great adventure so close to the start.

Erik nudges the boy. "Well, Sven! Have you something to say?"

Sven looks around, then meekly states, "I will take *The Trials*."

Sven winces slightly as Erik pulls his son's arm straight and draws a dagger. Erik cuts into the outer part of his son's forearm, making a shallow tear. Sven's blood drips slowly, pattering gently onto the stone floor, drop after drop.

"M-May I fight with honor or the rest of me follow," stutters Sven.

Elda pounds her staff on the floor with a thunderous hit. This action she repeats three times, stating, "Firstblood, may you lose yourself in struggle, then find yourself again, as a *Brond Here* of the Free North."

The *Brond* assembled grunt in agreement. Shouts of encouragement bubble up from the restless crowd as the possibility of more initiates stepping forward seems likely. Young prospects look around the room, measuring the competition while sizing up their chances.

Halmar says, "Remember Firstblood! A weapon does not a *Brond Here* make . . . a *Brond Here* is the weapon!"

Kare, Halmar's son, rises. He's a thick-waisted boy with hair the color of flame. Confident and strong, the boy speaks, "May I fight with honor or the rest of me follow."

Halmar bellows, "My son! The Eclipse begins soon. *Baldr* will not see you from his halls on *Iz*." He plays to the crowd. "But we can!"

The crowd eats his words up like a fresh leg of lamb, answering him with a cheer.

Halmar continues, "Make your deeds brave, and heart true. You'll finish this time, boy! I know it!"

The warriors grunt in agreement. Kare hears his father's last statement and winces; he would have preferred his past attempts be forgotten by the general crowd. Halmar passes his dagger down to the boy, who promptly does the blood rite. The hall cheers!

Marin rises next. A handsome girl of sixteen, she has an attractive face which marks a sharp contrast to her stocky figure, the athletic body of a shield-maid. Her pretty blonde hair is shorn down the sides, to give a more ferocious appearance.

"Marin, daughter of Nils, is unafraid!"

Nils crosses his arms.

Kare laughs. "Marin? Had I known this was a pie-baking fair, I would have brought my apron!"

Marin grabs him, twisting him back into a chokehold.

"Poor Kare. You didn't say you were hungry!"

She starts to force-feed Kare food from the table. The hall erupts with laughter.

"You see, Halmar? My daughter is more a son than yours!" Nils responds.

A HUGE LAUGH rips through the hall.

Marin drinks in the unexpected acceptance from the crowd. Kare, gasping for breath, taps her arm. He's had enough. Marin smiles and drops him to the floor as Nils passes her his dagger.

Erlann continues to watch from his chamber portal overlooking the hall.

With Excitement, he wheels toward Rolf and Red remarking, "The Trials! They're starting!"

Marin's voice floats up from below, "May I fight with honor or the rest of me follow."

Rolf tries to distract himself as he helps Red change into one of his robes.

"I care not." Rolf inspects Red. "The robes fit! You'll be the talk of *The Gathering*!"

Red inspects the garment. "Thank you, master Rolf."

Erlann replies, "We are all free men here, traveler."

Rolf jumps in and quips, "What Erlann is trying to say, is there are no masters in *Alstead*. No king, no queen; only the lands you keep, and those who defend it."

Red looks in the mirror. "No master . . . but myself."

Erlann marks Red, the boy's beginning to understand. "You can speak your mind and hold fast to it," says Erlann.

Red nods, straightening out his robe. He yanks the cloth down a little too violently, causing it to rip.

Rolf reacts. "Careful, boy! You ruined it!" He grabs onto Red, shaking him violently.

Erlann jumps to Red's defense, slicing between the two of them with his broad torso, ripping Rolf's arms from Red's shoulders. "Rolf! Stop this!" Erlann counters.

Rolf jabs his finger into Erlann's chest. "This is all your fault!" Rolf's eyes fill with a dagger of accusation, to which Erlann sharply returns his glare. Rolf continues, "If you hadn't fallen down that hole, we'd have been back sooner. Father would have never known!"

"Rolf?" Erlann's voice is full of confusion. *How could this possibly be my fault?*

Rolf grabs Erlann by the ears. "Shut it!"

Erlann stays silent, waiting for Rolf's boiling blood to cool. It works, he calms himself and releases Erlann. Without further word, Rolf crosses back to the portal window, looking down on the hall.

Rolf whispers to himself, though it matters not to him who hears, "I don't care what Father does to me! I will have a sword!"

Erlann understands. Rolf's angst is well-known to the youth of Northland. No one's name is written in the stones who hasn't first won his sword. To be denied an opportunity to prove one's mettle in *The Trials* is to be denied one's future. Erlann stands behind Rolf, feeling a fleeting moment of solidarity.

"Tell me not to go, and I will not."

Rolf clenches his fist. "Foolish brother. Father's angry with me, not you. Now go to it, before I hit you . . . hard."

Erlann knows Rolf speaks true. He quietly leaves his brother's side and exits the room.

CHAPTER 7

BY THEIR OWN CHOOSING

A very drunk Erik sits with Tyr. He's espousing his parental philosophy with passion. "Raising a son is like crafting a good sword. You have to bend them to your will, and yet, if you pull too hard, he breaks!"

The warriors grow silent as the doors of the hall open. Erlann works up the courage to approach the circle. As he takes the long walk to the center of the hall, his footsteps ring heavy on the stone.

"I am Erlann, grandson of the Once Queen Elda, son of *Brond Helm* Tyr, and I will take *The Trials*."

Silence, then Tyr speaks. "For song and glory?"

Erlann replies, "For the Free North. It's for the scalds to say what is worthy of honor."

A long quiet settles on the hall. Erlann waits, unsure of his father's next move. Tyr stands, studying him. After a moment, he nods and pulls his dagger. He passes it to Erlann by the blade. Erlann can tell by the look in Tyr's eyes that he has met with his father's approval. Then, he feels a pinch as he cuts into his own arm.

"May I fight with honor or the rest of me follow."

A cheer rings out in the hall.

Rolf slams his fist as he looks out onto the scene from his upper chamber.

Noticing his angst, Red moves alongside him and speaks, "In the old times, sons deemed unworthy of *The Trials* would steal upon the contest. There, with great deeds accomplished, their worth was proved."

Rolf notices something across the way in Tyr's room; it's the craftsfolk from before, still working tirelessly into the night. One of the craftsfolk's assistants sets down a new batch of eggs.

"And it was so." Rolf smiles.

Erlann looks up toward the portal window. With a guilty look in his eyes, he spies Rolf disappear from view.

Then, Erlann hears footsteps, the familiar clink and clank of scale armor and metal boots marching down the hall. It's a music all too familiar in the Northlands, a sound that harbingers menace.

Suddenly, an armed host pushes its way into the hall. Erlann notes that all the warriors of *Alstead* are defenseless, having already surrendered their swords to the lock and key. It's only the love of the spirit of *Baldr* and the fear of True Death that turns one from violence during the moons' eclipse. The defenseless host looks on as Axel and his men close in.

Elda rises from her seat among the *Brond*. "*Brond Helm* Axel. *The Gathering* has begun! Yet, you bear arms at the time when only words are to be spoken."

Axel's tired face is as weather-beaten as his breastplate, yet grim and determined. He speaks with an exhausted hoarse voice.

"Forgive me, Once Queen. There's a vile thing . . . a wolf that has come among your flock."

"There are no wolves here, friend," Elda says calmly. "Have you brought them with you?"

Erlann's gaze is immediately drawn to the girl by Axel's side. A stunning beauty with a haunted look in her eyes, she wears a runic necklace which, at first glance, appears to be broken in two. Erlann cannot make out the meaning of such a rune, incomplete as it is.

Just then, the amulet glows.

"Father!" Loa signals her Patriarch.

Axel turns to a man in a dark cloak sitting in the crowd, and says, "Animal! Where are you keeping him?" He glares. "Where is my son?"

Herald Egil, Ambassador of Thane, rises. A dark cowl covers his face, his shoulders are adorned by two wolf's heads that seem to snarl in contempt as he addresses the hall.

"He's safe, *Brond Helm* Axel, as long as I live."

Axel shouts, "Woe to the house of Thane that has stolen my son! Woe to the USURPER!"

The man in black leans forward casually. "We usurp? Accept Thane, your king!"

The other *Brond* rise, shouting and jeering at this absurd claim.

Tyr scoffs, "Your 'King' Thane has no more claim to kingship than anyone in this hall!"

"Thane is the true and only son of Queen Elda," Egil protests.

Elda breathes in, as the hall hangs on her every word. "I have but one son now, Herald." She places her hand on Tyr's back in affirmation. "He sits among his equals, a *Brond* of the Free North."

Herald Egil presses his master's claim, "A son through marriage, to a daughter long dead."

"Look around you, Herald." Elda cuts him off, "All who have joined us, I have adopted as my sons. For as long as these men hold to one another as brothers, what I have birthed here will never die."

Herald Egil grits his teeth.

"King Thane decrees, in the spirit of *The Gathering . . . Freya's rest.*"

The warriors of the hall grow silent.

Elda responds, "We are already at rest. It's forbidden to make war during the red eclipse; this is our oldest custom."

Egil continues, "In honor of these, our traditions, your true son, King Thane, would release all prisoners in his charge, as a gesture of unity."

Tyr snorts, "Another trick!"

Herald Egil addresses Tyr, "Your King only desires peace with the *Brond* of Northland and wishes to see all seven corners united once more."

Nils jumps in, "The Brond hold six of the seven corners already. Keep your seventh!"

The *Brond* laugh. Some pound the tables, and others shout insults. Elda holds up her hand, as the room grows silent yet again.

Tyr takes his cue and speaks. "Axel, of all the *Helms* of the North, your corner has the most broken shields and charred bones. What say you?"

Axel nods to Tyr, with his charge bordering the usurper, Thane, his people have seen the horrors of endless war. Though, he's appreciative of this chance to air his grievances.

"These days, it's the freedom of one man, my son, that I pine for the most."

Tyr takes the floor back, speaking broadly, "*Brond Helm*! No man has been more steadfast in this war against crowns."

Tyr raises his right hand. "In matters of this prisoner exchange, I move that we follow *Brond Helm* Axel's will and judgment."

Elda watches silently.

"So says I," Erik seconds.

"And I," agrees Nils.

The agreement continues around the hall as the other *Brond Helm* have their say. The vote terminates at the seventh corner, with Egil, who sits silently.

Elda whispers the ratification, "And it was so."

Axel moves toward Egil, who tenses at his approach. "My son is here. That much is true."

He looks at his daughter's glowing broken necklace. "Bring my son home to me and all the captive sons of Northland."

Egil rises. "Northland, prepare with joy for the return of your sons. Know that King Thane understands that the greatest sadness of all, is that of a family divided."

Axel grabs Egil. "Howl on, little wolf. But betray us, betray me, and True Death shall be yours. This I swear on *the spirit of Baldr*."

A Scald sings quietly in the corner:

"Oh light, where have you gone? Gone away, from the land."
"Oh warmth, where have you gone? Gone away, from his hand."
Everyone joins in:

"We drink to you! Baldr True; In death, our spirits lighten."
"May Freya's tears wash away; The blood of the titan."

The Brond of *Northland* return to the festivities as time marches on. Kare arm-wrestles *Brond Helm* Nils atop one of the tables. It's a hearty contest, one that Nils appears to be losing. Halmar excuses himself from the previous conversation to cheer for his son.

"Kare! Come on, son. Finish him!"

Nils seems to be running out of steam, "Ah . . . ah . . . Ha!"

Suddenly, Nils puts his full strength behind his arm, slamming Kare's arm onto the table.

"Better luck next span, boy!"

Halmar laughs. "No sons, Nils? Your boy would have won all *The Trials*!"

Nils looks at his daughter Marin, who is visibly offended by Halmar's comment. Nils waves off Halmar as Marin turns to Erlann, desperate to change the subject.

"You look fit, Erlann, since I saw you last."

"As do you, 'Shieldmaiden of Harr.'"

Marin smiles as she corrects him.

"*Brond Here*. I hope to be a *Brond Here* of Harr."

Erlann looks across the room and sees Loa sitting quietly. She looks out the window and mutters to herself as if memorizing the layout of the keep.

Kare smirks toward Erlann.

"Axel's daughter is beautiful," Kare says suggestively. "He keeps her close; I was beginning to think of her as a fiction."

Kare raises his mug as he studies Loa's figure.

"Trial or no, there's more than one way to prove yourself a man!"

Axel, who has been speaking with Tyr, catches the insinuation and is not amused. He swoops in, grabbing Loa's hand, and pulls her toward the door.

As they pass Erik, he asks, "*Brond Helm*? You'll not drink with us?"

Axel mournfully replies, "Till I embrace my son again, no *Brond Helm*, I will not."

Erlann watches after Axel and Loa as they swiftly exit the hall.

Night has come again. The flicker of torchlight dances across the walls of this great hall. As the fire pits burn their fuel down to ashes, starlight shines through the round smoke holes in the ceiling above. A scald sings drunkenly in the corner, reveling in quiet awe of *Rasmus's* creation.

Erlann surveys the room and notices that the *Brond Here* are scattered about in various states of drunkenness. Some snore loudly, some vomit their evening feast, but the overall energy of the hall has calmed greatly.

Erlann sees The *Horn of Hearth* sitting on the edge of the table, unattended. Carefully, he reaches for the horn, putting it to his lips:

The ground shakes as he begins to blow through the mouthpiece.

A hand drops on the top of the horn, stopping Erlann. The Caller has awakened.

"Lad, if I were you, I'd let that be."

Erlann realizes he's about to get himself into trouble, and mumbles, "Forgive me."

The Caller takes back the horn, being very careful to avoid its mouth.

"There is nothing to forgive."

Erlann admires the horn. "It's beautiful."

The Caller speaks. "The *Horn of Hearth*. Made by the same folks who forged your father's sword, I'd wager. Take my word . . ." The Caller leans in with his mead cup. "Anything made in the mountain is powerful, and should not be used lightly."

The Caller smiles at Erlann and returns to his drink.

CHAPTER 8

WHISPERS AND THE ONCE QUEEN

E rlann decides it's time for a long rest. He walks down the wide halls of *Stalden Keep*. Much like the city of *Alstead*, *Stalden's* wooden floors and stone walls wrap around into a circular ramp from floor to floor. It would be an infinite uphill battle for any would-be invader emerging from below. Then Erlann hears it, softly at first, as if the sandstone was whispering to him. No, not from the stones, but an ancient tongue, reverberating, penetrating through the rock. It's very close.

Erlann stops, listening harder. It's a woman's voice, speaking in *Storn Gar*, the language of the mountains. Erlann listens as he approaches the next room, and a cracked door.

"Espy Erlann? Ne?"

He hears his name, recognizing the unmistakable voice of his grandmother, Elda. Then, a different voice answers the first.

"Espy, aye."

Erlann peeks through an opening in the door. He sees his grandmother speaking with another woman, cloaked, and in secret.

Erlann whispers, *"The Men of the Mountains."* He turns from the door to sneak away.

Elda suddenly declares, "The *Stune Folc* are not fond of that name."

Erlann jumps! How did she know he was there?

As Erlann slowly opens the door, he sees that Grandmother is quite pleased with her little ambush.

She speaks with a self-satisfied tone, "Theirs was once a great empire on the surface, these *Stune Folc*. In the Northlands, Stalden itself was their fortress, but that was long ago."

The cloaked woman speaks perfectly in the language of the North, "Join us, Erlann."

A surprised Erlann is greeted by a woman in a full purple cloak. She bows her head, and Erlann nods in turn. Elda speaks, her voice carrying the tone of an introduction.

"She's impressed with you, Erlann. Few have looked into the eyes of the wolf and kept their life."

The cloaked woman speaks again, "It's as we have feared. Thane has breached the Isen Mur."

"The *Brond Here* of the Free North will stop him," Erlann responds proudly.

"I hope so, young Erlann," Elda states flatly, turning to the woman. "Erlann will begin *The Trials* tomorrow."

Erlann recites his education to the letter, "To be worthy in *Baldr's* eyes, all *Brond Here* must face True Death."

Erlann wishes to be brave, but he feels a wave of fear wash over his body. Those who succeed in *The Trials*, that is to say, those who demonstrate one of the virtues of *Baldr*, will win their sword. Granted the status of *Brond Here* in life, they'll be called to his great house on *Iz* after death. Failure means no sword in life, no life in death, but a death that is true and final.

Elda turns, and announces, "Lady Strongbridge, I would like to have words with my grandson."

The cloaked woman nods and looks at Erlann.

"*Staerd Stern*, Erlann."

Erlann does not understand. She speaks again.

"Greatness goes."

Erlann bows to the cloaked lady with respect and then follows Elda out of the room.

Down. Down. Down.

Down they walk into the depths of *Stalden Keep* and through the catacombs. As Erlann stumbles through the corridor, attempting to find his footing; Elda lifts a torch to bring more light. The cave looks almost natural except for the tiered shelves of the dead, carved into the stone by artisans with mallet and pick. A final mercy for the brave, shaped from the bosom of *Rasmus*.

Row after row of fallen warriors line the walls. These are the ancient *Stune Folc* warriors who fought for the keep in life and now support its base in death. Their shrines and markers are adorned with the best armor, shields, and blades one could afford—keeping vigil here in this place, for untold spans to come.

Erlann and Elda journey even deeper, to a much older part of the necropolis, whose halls are filled with ancient hordes and rooms reaching back to when the *Stune Folc* garrisoned there. Their final resting places lay undisturbed and respected by the *Brond Here* of *Alstead*. Erlann follows Elda toward two big doors at the end of the path. Erlann's shocked to discover his father's guards flanking the edifice on either side protecting it.

He stands amazed that anyone would be posted to such a place.

"Guards? Here?"

"Open," Elda commands.

The guards push on the giant doors as they swing inward, shrieking on rusty hinges.

Erlann stops, his face filling with apprehension. *What is this place?*

Elda looks impressed. "You are wise to hesitate."

"What's there?"

Elda looks past the doors, her voice fills with equal parts dread and mystery forming a riddle of her own. "Here rests a power that can twist proud warriors into slaves and corrode the best qualities of men. A greater evil I know not."

"I don't wish to see," mutters Erlann.

Elda fires back, "You wish to take your trials? Behold that which was my greatest test." She walks ahead, daring him to follow.

Erlann takes a moment to steel his courage and passes through the threshold. The doors seem to hover over his shoulders, caving in on him and creating an oppressive feeling. Inside, he sees a room that was once beautiful but has now fallen into dilapidation and decay. Columns line each side, and a long, rising staircase is flanked by rotting benches as it climbs up from the main floor. At its center, he discovers a throne.

The throne is overgrown with weeds that are slowly battling their way up through the floors. Natural light floods in from somewhere in the ceiling, revealing a crown. A beam shines upon it, which in turn rests on the throne in this once regal hall—as if placed there long ago and then forgotten.

"The crown of Northland!" exclaims Erlann.

"The only king to possess it turned out to be a queen," says Elda regretfully. "Look closer, Erlann."

As Erlann approaches the throne, a hand unexpectedly rakes at him from one of the side rooms, almost grabbing Erlann's shoulder. A prisoner, behind rusty bars and chained to the floor, extends his hand not in anger, but in a desperate plea for mercy.

"Please, boy, release me . . . wretched as I am!"

Erlann recognizes the man's clothing. "I know this one." Erlann's tone shifts to one of accusation, "You're one of Thane's men."

Elda says, "A prisoner of his 'king's' ambition. As he would shackle others to Thane's will, now he is shackled. A fitting demise for a fool."

Erlann hears a multitude of voices calling out from the adjoining rooms. He realizes this place, once the royal seat of Northland, now chambers the usurper's men as a petty dungeon. The prisoners' voices raise into a cacophony of desperation. Behind the clattering of corroding bars, they shout and beg for release.

Elda hisses, "Silence, traitors!"

The prisoners go quiet. A pin could drop on the floor, and it would resonate through the room as clearly as a man's neck being chopped on the headsman's block.

Elda speaks again, with a curse on her lips, "You may soon be released, but you will never know freedom."

Erlann advances toward the crown positioned at the head of the throne room. As he progresses, he loses sight of the prisoners, their view obscured by the stone columns.

Taken in, he reaches for the crown, and says out loud. "How could such a small thing lead men to betrayal?"

Elda watches him and whispers, "If our kin of Northland are to remain free, be he friend or foe, all who would wear this crown must die!"

Erlann's hand enters the beam of light. Suddenly, huge razor-sharp blades, like claws, pop out from the throne, rotating and spinning. Erlann pulls back before the blades can take his hand clean off.

The spinning blades wind down, halting their motion, as the prisoners hold in place behind bars. Time has paused again, it seems, like down by the river. Nothing moves as the last sounds made hang perpetually in the air.

Erlann jumps and curses at the same time, *"Freya's tears!"*

Erlann breathes heavily as Elda levels a dagger to his throat. She's unaffected by the machinations of time around them. She speaks with fear in her voice.

"We have both looked into the eyes of the wolf and seen the future."

Elda's eyes darken as she runs the blade down his shoulder.

She turns the blade into Erlann's arm, nicking him. Erlann's blood falls to the floor, forming a puddle of crimson. Then, Elda forces Erlann to the ground. His face is so close to the puddle that he can see his own reflection in it.

But his reflection is older, as it was in the ice cave. His older self gazes back with gray hair and an evil eye. Erlann observes in horror as his future self places the crown on his head.

"The end of all things," Elda continues, "begins with you!"

Elda forces his face into the puddle, breaking the surface. Down into the widening darkness, in a space between the reflection that Erlann knows and the infinite actions of the people of *Rasmus*—Erlann looks down into the nebula of existance, infinite in horizon as it is deep.

Erlann peers into the nearby clouds. He sees ancient wars and strange arcane technologies momentarily illuminated in the lightning of this gap.

Erlann gasps, and chokes, "What is this place?"

"Echoes of the past and whispers of the future. All that was and all that ever could be, churns here in a single moment, in this Great-In-Between."

Erlann looks down into the infinite storm, clouds of Tyr, Thane, Rolf,

Marin—everyone he knows and many more he doesn't. The clouds begin to churn, faster and faster.

"Behold, Erlann, the King of Northland!" Elda pronounces.

Erlann watches in horror as his older self cuts the great chain in two, unleashing Fenreir. A great battle begins. A mighty host gathers behind Erlann to battle death itself. Marin and many others cheer with swords raised as they charge.

Young Erlann watches as his host of warriors is overwhelmed by a legion of *Vuloospa*. They fight hard but are going down by the hundreds.

Elda shouts, "This will be!"

Marin is impaled on a spear, a gruesome battlefield death.

"This will be!"

Older Erlann is knocked from his horse by Fenreir. Erlann closes his eyes as his older self is mauled to death.

"Stop this! Stop!!!!!" Erlann protests.

Erlann is bombarded with images of Fenreir consuming the world of *Rasmus*. He tries to pull his face from the puddle, but Elda holds him down, trying to drown him.

"You have seen the darkness of Isen Mur. Fenreir still lives. His hunger can never be unleashed."

Erlann closes his eyes and reaches out. In this place, time does not exist. He can reach out to his grandmother's mind, connecting to her through this singularity of being.

Erlann pleads, "Grandmother, if I'm to die, then let it be as a *Brond Here*. That I may join my mother in the *Halls of Iz*."

Elda considers Erlann's well-spoken words.

She loosens her grip, allowing Erlann to gasp for air. He falls back onto the floor, his eyes bloodshot and burned through his blood-soaked skin. He's paralyzed with sheer astonishment, unable to move or speak after what he's seen, laying there motionless as tears roll down his cheek.

Elda softens, saying, "Once again, my daughter has given you life. But know this, a king's life you SHALL NEVER HAVE."

CHAPTER 9

COVENANT OF BROND

In the forbidden marsh, in a place that's scarcely more than an outpost on the outskirts of *Alstead*, a lone *Brond Here* patrols the pass. His gaze extends toward the imposing walls of *Stalden Keep* in the far distance. They're stunning. With a nod, he acknowledges the beauty of the morning.

A twig snaps prompting the guard to turn abruptly as a war hammer crashes into him, instantly shattering his windpipe. The guard gasps for breath, clutching his crushed throat. He desperately reaches toward the distant city. He must warn them! He must sound the alarm! But no noise comes as his remaining strength leaves him. Staggering, gasping, the *Brond Here* collapses onto the dusty road. His desperate eyes focus on the spires of *Stalden Keep* rising above the protective outer walls. It's out of reach now, he laments, no warning will come.

Thane steps into the daylight, his visage covered in crimson splatter.

He declares, "The city of *Alstead*. Where all men speak their mind and hold fast to it."

Thane's men emerge from their hiding places in the dark underbrush, joining him as he studies the approach to *Alstead*. They're Thane's Vanguard, his *Stafntaki*. One of the men, Thane's captain, stands in the front rank awaiting orders. He's a large man in his own right whose armor is scarred from countless battles, but not more than his face. The captain's face is a map of war and torture, a history of endless violence carved by both rivals—and comrades.

The captain observes the choking guard, "This one must be of the quiet sort, then."

He smirks, approaching the *Brond Here*. "Well, speak your mind?"

Thane's captain hovers over the *Brond Here* with a sadistic smile. "What's that? Speak up, boy!"

The *Brond Here* gargles with labored breath, but no words come.

Thane ignores the captain's petty display and waves to someone down the road. A rumble is heard, and several wagons emerge from the marsh, rolling toward the city of *Alstead*.

Thane turns and asks, "Everything's prepared?"

The captain hops up, proclaiming, "Prisoners, ha! Who would pine for the return of their weakest warriors?"

Thane casts the captain an angry look.

The captain swallows his words. "All is ready, my King."

Thane kneels down next to the dying *guard*. He looks into the *Brond Here's* panicked eyes as the two men share an unexpected and intimate moment.

"I was once as you are now. Abandoned and alone in the midst of my enemies. My mother left me this hammer. It was her last gift to me. I am told she has found her 'law.' but now . . ."

Thane palms a vial, which hangs around his neck. It's a glass tube with a silver top in the shape of a wolf's head which is filled with Fenreir's blood, that he and his men collected from the cold dark of *Isen Mur*.

"I have found mine. Go now to your *Halls of Iz*, without shame."

The guard takes his last dying breath as Thane crouches next to him. The *Brond Here's* convulsions slow as his body goes still. Lo', his pupils relax into a sightless death.

Thane smears his fingers through the blood on the war hammer. He begins an incantation as his captain watches in a trancelike state.

"With hunger, as the wolf, I devour my prey."

". . . as all will be devoured," Thane's captain finishes.

Slowly, Thane pulls his thumb down his forehead, leaving a bloody mark in the shape of a sharp slash. Then, he reaches for the captain's forehead and repeats the mark. As Thane bloods his warriors, the caravan thunders past; one wagon after another rolls in an almost endless procession.

As the last wagon passes, Thane grabs hold of it and swings up next to the driver. Dozens of wagons roll toward *Alstead* and its commanding heights. Thane glares upward to the formidable spires of *Stalden Keep*.

"Your son returns, Once Queen. Soon your trials begin."

Ensam Fjall, a lonely mountain, stands on the outskirts of *Alstead*—it's a place where scouts keep watch on the eastern seas and western approaches. Where, a swift message from carrier falcons guarantees that no armies may march on the northeast corner of Northland without being spotted, and the *Brond Here* host alarmed.

Today, however, the watchman's redoubt serves a different purpose. The excitement of the crowd is palpable as the eclipse begins. The twin moons of *Iz* and Brond hang close together, overlapping in the early morning sky. The first trial will commence soon. Erlann walks toward the starting line, passing Elda, who stands among the crowd. They lock eyes for a moment, and he continues on.

Erlann is exhausted. He's a complete wreck from the night before, with bloodshot eyes and matted hair. Stumbling forward, he sizes up the competition. One boy meditates on the virtues of *Baldr*, while another stretches his arms in physical preparation. As Erlann walks, an old familiar face turns around—it's the *First Spear* from the parapet. Erlann can tell from the old warrior's smirk, that the game is spent.

"Too much drink last night?" the old warrior jests. "Luck, boy!"

Erlann ignores him as he weaves through the crowd. He discovers Loa standing by; she's tapping the rune amulet with her hands. It's no longer glowing. For a brief moment, they make eye contact. Erlann acknowledges Loa as he takes his place on the starting line.

It seems that every family of Northland is present today. Parents stand behind their children, offering last-minute advice and guidance. Most of the initiates are boys, but several girls are also present, as well as a sizable minority of young adults repeating *The Trials*.

Brond Helm Nils speaks to his daughter, Marin. Using broad gestures, he shares a war story. *Brond Helm* Erik stands with Sven, his son, coaching him as well.

"True warriors never fail . . ."

"T-they find a way," responds Sven.

Kare, in conversation with Halmar, notices Sven's stutter. He makes a mocking face toward Sven.

Erik pulls Sven's attention back to him, saying, "I have carried this shield into many battles. It will protect you, as it did my father and father's father before."

Sven nods with intensity, trying to show his bravery.

Tyr stands by the starting line also, nodding to Erlann as he cracks his knuckles. Erlann begins to speak, but Tyr raises his hand, stopping him.

"Now is the time for doing," Tyr says firmly.

Erlann nods to his father.

The Horn of Hearth sounds in the air!

Gong . . . gong . . . Erlann hears a strange sound that he's not familiar with.

It's some kind of bell, with a tone that rings soft and deep, yet it resonates throughout the many surrounding hills. Erlann looks into the mist. Slowly, a mysterious figure emerges.

From what Erlann can tell, it's the woman from last night. She's covered from head to toe in a travel robe woven in the fabled under-place of *Stor Doren*. Lady Strongbridge stands for a moment inspecting the initiates—she's flanked by two other robed men who stand beside her. The crowd is awed by the sight of her.

One man *whispers, "The Men of the Mountains."*

The three *Stune Folc* stand by a stone forge that's dimly lit with the flickering glow of a nearby fire, its smoke dancing in the cold mountain air. The redoubt walls, rough-hewn from ancient stone, are etched with fading runes. Shadows play across the space, stretching from the stone overlook to the altar at the center, where an intricate array of tools are set—a quiet testament to the superior craftsmanship of the Stor Doren Blacksmiths. The rhythmic crackling of the fire is the only sound, broken by the occasional hissing of the wind.

The lady speaks. "Children of the Free North, inheritors of The Seven Corners, hear these words . . ."

The other two figures lower their hoods and head for the forge. A blacksmith and his apprentice. The master's gait is steady, deliberate, with a quiet strength in every movement. He approaches the forge with practiced ease, his rough hands pulling a hot metal shard from the fire, its orange glow illuminating the worn lines of his face. As the blacksmith places the shard upon the altar, cold stone meets molten metal with a quiet hiss.

"*Brond*," Erlann mutters in recognition of the element.

Sven turns his head, listening.

"The metal of the mountains," Erlann explains with deep reverence.

The blacksmith hammers at his station as the dark fire of the *Brond* moon eclipses the icy light of *Iz*. Lady Strongbridge speaks after each strike of the hammer.

"*Fidelity*."

The hammer hits.

Someone in the crowd points to the moons as the sky grows darker.

"*Hospitality*."

Hit.

"*Industriousness*."

Hit.

"*Discipline*."

Hit.

Erlann feels someone staring at him from behind. He turns to glimpse Rolf, who's in a disguise of his own—a thick rain slicker covers him from head to toe. Unnoticed, he works his way through the crowd disappearing into a sea of attendees.

"*Perseverance*."

Hit.

"*Self-Reliance*."

Hit.

The moon's shadow eclipses Kare.

"*Truth*."

Hit.

The moon's shadow eclipses Marin.

"*Courage.*"

Hit.

The moon's shadow eclipses Sven.

"*Honor.*"

The moon's shadow eclipses Erlann.

Hit.

"Since the dawning, nine swords of *Brond* have been given in these trials. Nine for each of the virtues we saw in *Baldr the cold-bringer*. For, as he brought pain to the world, now you must struggle. This is what it means to be a *Brond Here* of Northland."

Erlann notices Elda standing on the sidelines, waiting for *The Trials* to begin. Known throughout as the Once Queen of Northland, she had been Erlann's grandmother and teacher all of his days. As the tutor of the Sons of Tyr, she instructed Erlann on lessons of old and always cautioned Rolf to think before doing. She would playfully accuse Erlann of jumping ahead of her instruction, of knowing her mind, but would then somehow always regain the lead. Today, though, things feel more like an ending than a beginning for Erlann. Elda's expression is stern and impenetrable as dark obsidian; her gaze as icy as *Iz* itself.

Lady Strongbridge continues. "If any child who would return home to mother and hearth, go now . . . no shame will follow you."

Kare tosses a rock which bounces off the back of Sven's helmet.

Sven turns to see Kare standing over him with a nasty smirk on his lips.

Kare speaks with a mocking tone, "T-T-Try not to piss yourself . . . *Firstblood.*"

The boys laugh. Erlann looks at Kare, annoyed.

Marin fires back, "Shut it, *Vein Clot.*"

The boys now snicker at Kare, a clever reversal.

Kare's face turns red at this obvious insult as Marin mocks him for repeating the trials.

He demands, "What did you call me, girl?"

Marin isn't intimidated, as she touts, "How many trials have you failed, Kare?"

Kare's eyes turn bloodshot with anger. He sneers at her and says, "*The Trials* are masked from *Baldr's* sight. He won't miss one little girl."

Marin meets his gaze, and in a sing-song voice, she says, "See you on the mountain, Kare."

Then, Erlann speaks with a quiet authority, "Marin. Kare. Put this aside, for today we face the greatest enemy we will ever face."

Marin knows this to be the case, "*True Death*. If we die today, our spirits will be lost forever in The Great In-Between."

The other boys shrink back, considering.

"Let us focus on *The Trials* ahead," Erlann explains with empathy in his voice.

"Come and stand with me, Sven."

In this moment, Erlann glances at Tyr from the corner of his eye. He crosses his arms, impressed with his son. Erlann's fear transmutes into a wave of pride that swells up from his heart. His father's approval comes less often than the eclipse on *Rasmus* and is never spoken. Yet, there's a glow in his father's eye when Erlann has done well—like a hidden flame, illuminating a bond that only a father and son can share.

Erlann notices Sven gripping his father's shield protectively. "My father told me, 'live or die', he will be proud that I stood on this day.'"

Erlann nods at Sven, and then looks upward toward the heights. A morning mist rolls in, drifting across the wooded, stony peaks, and then clears, revealing their course for the day. It's an old stone path. Not a path where stones are brought and laid, but a path cut into the face of the mountain itself. Shaped in times before reckoning and worn down by a sum of countless feet upon its rock, the old, eroded path shines in the twilight of the moon's eclipse.

The mountain is separated from the starting line by a den of boulders, which the children will have to navigate their way down and then back up the mountain peak, somehow.

From her place at the starting line Lady Strongbridge holds up a large spotted egg.

Erlann and Marin can't hide their concern. That's no falcon egg, nor does it have the likeness of any egg they have ever seen. It's much bigger, covered in hair and sharp barbs—ferocious in appearance to be sure.

Marin asks, "What manner of beast laid that?"

Lady Strongbridge responds, "Keep your spirit, and the first sword, that of *Fidelity*, shall be yours."

The blacksmith holds up a super-heated sword blade with his tongs. Sven finds his confidence, and says, "I shall be the first to have it!"

"Says the 'coward' who hides behind his shield!" Kare needles.

Erlann sighs. *No one ever seems to listen, at any age.*

Lady Strongbridge finishes, "To those who would be *Brond Here*, return with an egg, or not at all."

The horn sounds.

"Begin!"

The *Brond* and their assorted families let out a bold cheer of encouragement. The children growl with sound and fury as they charge through the mud toward the den of boulders. But some children are faster than others. One boy trips out in front of Erlann, who quickly jumps over him as the boy lands, eating a face full of mud. Erlann does all this while pulling Sven along by the collar after him. The pack of boys begins to separate as the mud sticks to their shoes.

Erlann encourages his neighbor, "Don't stop, Sven!"

They reach the edge of the den of boulders and begin their descent. As Erlann climbs down the outcropping he looks up and sees Sven, hovering at the very top.

"Hurry, Sven!"

Sven looks back at the crowd, to the families looking on, to his father Erik watching him with concern. Sven realizes it's too early to fall this far behind. He's paralyzed with shame.

Erlann calls to him, "Sven! You wish to make your father proud? To be great, like him?" Erlann grabs his full attention. "Greatness goes! We need to go!"

Sven understands, it's as if a new focus washes over him. He repeats the phrase over and over, like an incantation and begins to climb down, chanting, "Greatness goes. Greatness goes."

Suddenly, his leg slips from the rock; it finds a new foothold on top of Erlann's hand.

"Careful!" Erlann encourages him, while reacting to the pain.

Sven apologizes, "I'm sorry! I'm sorry!"

Erlann pushes Sven's foot back into the rock face. "Get a hold. Good."

They both climb down together as Erlann jumps onto a ledge, followed by Sven.

"See that rock?"

Sven sees it and nods. "Like a bridge, isn't it?"

"Go!" Erlann instructs.

The two boys run across the rock outcropping. The other initiates look up and realize they are taking the longer way across! They begin to backtrack, following Erlann and Sven as they make their way up *Ensam Fjall*.

CHAPTER 10

THE SHOULDER OF RASMUS

Erlann, cut and bruised by hours of climbing, breaks above the mist and rolls up onto the summit. He looks out over Northland. Though exhausted and gasping for breath, he's at once amazed by what he sees. They're above the clouds now, which form a misty blanket almost like another ground in the sky.

Erlann conjures up a second wind of energy and leaps to his feet, exclaiming, "Sven, we've made it!"

He reaches for Sven, who's panting with exhaustion as he pulls him up to the relative safety of the out-cropping. They rest for a moment as Sven looks over the side. "The mist is so thick . . . I can hardly see the ground!" Erlann stares in awe. "That's no mist, my friend . . . today we sit on the shoulders of *Rasmus*."

They both laugh and take a moment, running their hands through the clouds. Below, Erlann can see all the corners of Northland and some of the Burning South beyond. Its mountains and tundras, lakes, marshes and woodlands carpet the land below. It's clear to Erlann why this is the first test—to show *fidelity* for all of Northland and its peoples below.

Erlann rises, seeing something. He points a finger at Sven.

"Quiet!"

The cloud they have found themselves in, passes by the summit. As the vapor clears, giant nests are revealed in the rock outcroppings of the mountain. This is their goal! They run up to the first nest. Erlann confirms it: the spotted eggs are inside.

Sven's eyes fill with concern. "They're so big! How will we climb back down?"

Erlann looks around the bottom of the nest; it's a carefully constructed weave of twigs, grass, and leaves. A thought builds in his mind.

"Grab the straw."

Sven nods in agreement.

They weave the straw as tightly as they can, and then they pack it tighter. Erlann and Sven make a crude basket from the available materials.

Whoooosh!

In the mist, they hear something slicing through the air like an arrow with an unbearable hiss. Erlann marks the sky with apprehension. He thinks, *Nothing on wings should be able to move this quickly.*

Whoooosh!!!

Sven turns his head, "What was that?"

Erlann pulls Sven back to the task at hand. "Quickly, help with these."

Erlann picks up an egg and stuffs it into the makeshift basket. Whatever that thing is, it won't suffer them to pass.

Sven peels his gaze away from the sky and grabs for a second egg. Suddenly, he winces.

"Ouch!" He drops the egg back into the nest. "It cut me!"

Erlann looks at Sven's hand, now dripping with blood. The boys turn back to the egg, a single crack in its shell multiplies into another crack, and then another.

Erlann studies the egg with mounting concern. "Sven, step back!"

It's hatching. Sven turns to see the other eggs beginning to crack open as well.

"Erlann, look!"

Erlann watches as a razor-sharp beak punches through the shell. An eagle-shaped head emerges from inside, taking its first breath in this world.

Sven, amazed at this discovery, blurts out, "A most beautiful bird! Erlann, look!"

Erlann shrinks with horror. "That's no bird!"

As the rest of the eggs hatch, the little chick scratches at Sven with a paw—a lion's paw.

Erlann grabs Sven, yelling, "Hurry!"

They hear the shouts of other boys as they reach the top. The initiates have caught up with Erlann and Sven. The race is on to loot the eggs from the remaining nests.

Whoosh!

Something flies by again, too quickly to see.

Erlann loses his calm, "Sven! We have to go! Now!"

"Give me the egg!" Sven retorts with a rage that surprises Erlann.

Stunned, Erlann looks and sees one unhatched egg in the nest. "Get that one!"

As Sven reaches for his prize, two initiates come out of nowhere and grab the egg. They laugh while one of them taunts him, saying, "Too slow, Sven!"

"See you at the bottom!" says the second one.

SKREEEEE!!!!!!

Suddenly, a huge mother griffin swoops down from the sky onto one of the initiates, crushing him. She ROARS again.

Her voice is a mash between an eagle's cry and a lion's roar. She lifts the second initiate with her paws embedded deeply in his chest. The boy drops the egg screaming in pain. The mother griffin clutches him and flies out over the edge, taking him into the mist and . . . drops him. The child's blood-curdling scream is heard as he falls through the clouds to his death on the hillside below.

Erlann points to the newly available egg resting on the edge of the cliff. "Sven!!!"

Sven's eyes seem to bulge out of his head as he charges for the unclaimed egg, but the chicks give chase pecking at his hands, head, and all around his body as he tries to reach for the egg.

"Ouch!"

"Ouch!"

The baby griffons almost seem to laugh at him, *if baby griffons could laugh*, thinks Erlann.

"Stop it!" Sven lashes back as he tries once again to grab for the egg. Finally, Sven scoops it up.

Erlann looks skyward as another giant griffin lands in front of the nest. It holds a baby calf in its mouth and hisses with rage at the intruders.

Sven shouts, *"Freya's tears!"* as he backs up with the egg in his arms.

The mother griffin follows him with her head slowly. It's a standoff; she's looking for her chance to strike.

"Nice birdie, nice birdie," Sven chants as he puts the egg back in the nest.

"Sven!" Erlann says through gritted teeth. "Don't. Move."

Sven freezes in terror, confronted by the very real possibility of his imminent death.

It's in this moment, Erlann has a thought. He studies the shield on Sven's back; it's a very large shield, like a pair of pants three sizes too big.

"Sven, hang on!"

Erlann charges, throwing the full weight of his body into Sven, knocking them both off the edge of the cliff. Sven screams as he lands on his back, his shield skipping across the snow with several thuds, releasing a storm of powder that whips against their faces. It's working! The boys slide down the mountain slope on the back of Sven's shield. With the basket and egg on Sven's chest, Erlann steers the shield as he would a sled, pulling his arms up or down to avoid rocks and drop-offs in their way. Sven screams in sheer terror! It's incredibly distracting to Erlann as he negotiates the turns; the two boys are face-to-face, rocketing down the snowy slope.

A large group of onlookers waits at the finishing line, with the *Brond Helm* standing in a place of honor up front. *Brond Helm* Erik notices a trail of powder descending from the mountain at an alarming speed.

"Avalanche!"

Murmurs of concern escalate to full-blown panic as the onlookers clamor and cry in dreadful commotion. Tyr rises and looks upon the mountainside.

"Stop!" he says, signaling to the others. "Look!"

Tyr points to the boys as they emerge from the trail of snow. Erlann and Sven, gaining speed, head toward the den of boulders at the starting line.

Erlann holds tightly to the shield, lowering himself as much as possible.

"Hang on!" He dodges each incoming branch and stone with artful agility, but they just keep coming in faster succession as the forest thickens toward the bottom of the mountain.

Erlann turns again to avoid an oncoming log, but as they do so, the two boys don't see a rock partially obscured in the snow. More ramp than rock, it changes their course, launching them upward into the sky. As they fly over the edge, shield spinning, Erlann sees a rocky grave waiting below. The sound of wind rushes in Erlann's ears as they vault through the clouds.

Then, all the noise melts away. There's an eerie quiet as their momentum shifts. In this moment between up and down, life and death, there's a stillness as gravity takes hold. Erlann knows their path is set now.

"We've failed."

Sven is too terrified to say anything.

"Sven, prepare yourself," Erlann speaks calmly.

Even though he knows that Baldr cannot see him beneath the eclipse, Erlann prays anyway. To def ears, he prays. His voice is low, shaking at first, but each word gathers strength as he continues..

Erlann prays, "Hail *Baldr*, titan, bringer of cold, from you all good is known . . ."

Sven joins him. "Bring us, young and old, through breaking blow; home to your fold."

The attendees at the finishing line look up and point in horror as Erlann and Sven fall from a great height. Erik turns to Tyr whose body tenses at the realization that nothing more can be done. Erlann and Sven repeat the chant over and over as they drop from the sky.

Elda stands calmly in the hysterical crowd. Unnoticed, she radiates with a sad determination. She closes her eyes in resignation.

Erlann closes his eyes as well, awaiting the final crash. But death does not come, only a gentle . . . THUD.

They've stopped falling, or something has stopped them from falling. Sven is the first to slowly open his eyes.

"Erlann! Look!" The clouds separate, revealing the mother griffin.

She holds them up with Sven's shield in her talons, and with it, the two boys. The griffin looks at Erlann with what might be considered a smile. She appears to be saving them.

"What's this?" gasps Erlann.

Sven celebrates and pumps his fist as they fly past the disbelieving crowd, which erupts into cheers at the finishing line. Erlann looks back toward the den of boulders as they sail past. They're well ahead of the other boys, even with this detour.

Elda meets Erlann and Sven as they land safely in front of the finishing line. She pauses for a moment. Closing her eyes as she approaches the griffin, connecting her mind to the beast.

Erlann speaks with absolute bewilderment, "Grandmother. Why? Why did she catch us?"

Elda says, "She watched you climb from the foot of the mountain. She admires your *Fidelity*. To your comrade, Sven. To the spirit of *Baldr*."

"It's your loyalty to the things you love. She finds this beautiful and worth saving."

Erlann's at a loss for words as Elda smiles with pride. She turns back toward the mother griffin, who gently shudders at her touch.

"Be at peace now. Your pride has been saved. Your children shall be returned."

The griffin blinks. A calm runs through her as Elda runs a hand through her feathers. The two boys jump to the ground, but as Erlann lands, he slips. The egg slides from his basket, skids across the snow, and smashes on the ice.

"The egg has been placed," announces Lady Strongbridge.

Her words weigh heavily on Erlann as their reality sinks in. Someone has won, which means after all his tribulations this day, Erlann has failed the trial—this chance has been lost. The sound of laughter and thunderous applause is heard. Crushed, Erlann turns to honor the victor. But he's not prepared for what he sees next. It's Rolf who stands before the crowd at the altar—having placed the egg upon the stone.

Rolf? Erlann thinks to himself. *What evil trick is this?* Red stands next to Rolf, smirking and applauding his patron.

Tyr slams his fist down on a nearby table, breaking it with his sheer strength. Stone-faced, he walks away from a confused crowd struck by his actions. Erlann looks on with concern. His brother has never defied their father so directly before.

Red breaks the awkward silence and shouts, "A *Brond Here* is made this day! Glory! Glory to the house of Stalden!"

Erlann turns toward the den of boulders as Kare emerges over the top with his egg, and a devastated look on his face. Marin follows behind, struggling to grab a handhold of rock. Everyone's exhausted from this day's trial. Kare shrugs at Marin; they've all lost this challenge anyway. He reaches out to her. She marks his face for sincerity and then allows him to pull her to the top.

At the altar, everyone in attendance witnesses Lady Strongbridge present Rolf with his first sword. Silver and black, the runic word for *Fidelity* is carved into its blade. Rolf holds up the shining sword to an admonishing crowd.

"And it was so!" Lady Strongbridge exclaims.

Rolf basks in the glorious moment that he has so long desired.

CHAPTER 11

THE BROKEN AND THE BRAVE

As the *Men of the Mountains* collect the unplaced eggs from the other initiates, Erlann sulks through the vacating crowd. The onlookers return to the city of *Alstead* in a steady stream, while a few vendors remain behind packing their wares. Suddenly, one of Strongbridge's attendants drops something.

Erlann reacts, saying, "Hold on. You've dropped a—"

He stops in place, remembering that by law, he cannot touch a sword. Strongbridge's servant picks up the weapon instead.

"You did well today, Erlann, son of Tyr," says Lady Strongbridge.

Erlann broods. "All of that, to fail in the end."

"There are many more trials left. Many more chances for victory. You still live. Most would say that being alive is necessary to achieve victory," grins Strongbridge.

Erlann studies her face. *Is she joking? They're so difficult to read, these Men of the Mountains.* Erlann reckons there's truth in her words, either way. His heart feels even heavier when he looks across the way. He sees Elda, whispering into the ear of the mother griffin whose egg Erlann broke upon the ground. The servants of Strongbridge tenderly place the collected eggs on the spires of the altar as an entire flock of griffins swoop down from the sky. They gently lift the remaining eggs in their mouths and take flight, returning to the slopes of *Ensam Fjall*.

Erlann notices that one egg remains on the altar—the egg that had been Rolf's. Erlann's face grows stern with realization as he looks at Rolf's left hand. There's peeling flakes of dry paint on it . . . the same color as the griffin's eggs.

Erlann storms toward Rolf, grabbing his hand.

"ROLF! YOU CHEATED!"

"Did I?" Rolf violently pushes Erlann against the tent.

"You DARE challenge my honor? Do you?"

Red looks around for eavesdroppers, but none of the remaining folk notice them. Rolf dips his hands into a water bowl. The paint runs off his fingers, turning the water into a murky fog, and with it the evidence of his transgression. Rolf holds his clean hand up to Erlann's face.

Red plays along with a mischievous grin.

"Today, your brother has won the sword of *Fidelity*. Are you not proud of him?"

Erlann regrets befriending this runaway on the banks of the *Grenileir*.

"Your part in this is known to me."

Red smirks, lifting his finger to his lips. "Shhhhhh!"

Back at *Stalden Keep*, Erlann nurses his bruised bones as he walks gingerly down the hall. As his feet scrape the stone, he perceives the moans and screams of the wounded. Erlann enters the keep's infirmary, where several *Daughters of Freya* tend to the wounded. Many boys and girls with varying degrees of injury are crowded into beds and chairs, making the large room seem small in capacity. One healer wraps a boy's head with a bandage; it's clear the child has lost his sight.

A strong, deliberate voice cuts through the noise. It's a healer, a priestess of *Freya*.

She says quietly, "Tap it."

A *Brond Here* hammers on the sharp side of a griffon's talon. He gently taps out a piece of the claw that has gone through and broken off inside the arm of a wounded initiate.

"Tap it."

"Hold him. Hold him," says another healer.

Another *Brond Here* holds the wounded boy down as she applies water from the *Grenileir*. The boy screams on contact as another healer wipes her hands.

She laments, "Another day, another trial begins."

Erlann looks down at another boy whose gaze is returned with lifeless eyes.

It's *True Death*.

The unseeing corpse stares blankly up at Erlann as his eyes are closed by a healer, who gives Erlann an apologetic glance. The priestess speaks to Erlann.

"Come then. Let's have a look at you."

Erlann looks around the room at the other battered initiates and feels ashamed to count his wounds among theirs. He waves off the healer and heads for the door, but then he hears his father's voice.

"Good healers, do you want for anything?"

Erlann sees Tyr lurking in the doorway. He has to bend down slightly to fit through.

The healer responds, "Many lives were saved by this water. Thanks to you for bringing it, *Brond Helm*."

Erlann swells with pride seeing this side of his father that he has never known until this moment. They walk together back into the hall.

Erlann speaks with hesitation. "Would it be wrong . . . to wish these trials over?"

Tyr replies, "You would have your sword simply given to you? What value would that hold? And what of your next challenge? The next after?"

Rolf appears down the hall and quickly stops in his tracks. In that same moment, Erlann sees him as well but discreetly ignores him. He can see the look on Rolf's face, and Erlann immediately knows what his brother is thinking.

What are they talking about?

Rolf glares at Erlann with suspicion as Tyr continues, "There will always be trials in life, son. They shape us, mold us . . ."

Erlann listens.

"You can only know yourself, through becoming."

Erlann takes his place on the starting line of *Perseverance*. He looks upward into a giant hedge with pillars of stone. Erlann sees the *First Spear*, who stands atop the entrance of the maze with a whip in his hand.

He smiles at Erlann. It's time for a little payback.

A horn sounds! The *First Spear* cracks his whip at Erlann as the boys run past into a giant hedge maze. Several older men stand on top of the hedges with bullwhips. They're positioned at the dead ends and sides, whipping anyone unfortunate enough to stray too close.

The horn sounds again! The trial is over. A boy holds up his new sword with a triumphant smile, He's covered in lash marks from shoulder to waist. Erlann notices Rolf, who smirks at him from the sidelines holding his sword.

Erlann takes his spot on the next starting line: *Hospitality*. It's a drinking competition. All the fathers cheer on their sons as one boy passes out and falls to the ground. Out of the corner of his eye, Erlann sees that most of the other boys have either quit or have doubled over sick. One incredibly slovenly boy remains, drinking down the mead like a fish gobbling for breath.

Erlann can't help it; he's going to be sick.

The slovenly boy holds up his new sword.

Next, Erlann sits at the long table of *Industriousness*—building a homemade weapon out of the pieces supplied for him on the table. The initiates tap and carve stones from scratch, shaping primitive blades. Red sits next to Erlann, assembling his charge very quickly.

Feeling the pressure, Erlann and Sven rush to finish, hurling their hastily constructed daggers at the targets—Erlann's lands a little off-center, while Sven's bounces off the target and falls to pieces. Red answers their effort with his completed axe, and a toss that hits dead-center on the target.

"And it was so . . ." Red says mockingly as he holds up his new sword.

Another boy holds up the sword of *Discipline*.

Another, the sword of *Courage*.

Then, Erlann splashes into the water of *Self-Reliance*—a swimming competition. Suddenly, another boy jumps right on top of him, pushing him under. Erlann's legs and arms scrape across the riverbed, tearing his skin on the sharp stones below. He braces his legs against the bottom and shoves back toward the surface, launching the boy into the air. Erlann gasps for breath as his face breaks through the water. Panting, he looks down the river, but the other initiates have moved too far ahead. Rolf and Red laugh from the sidelines, holding their swords.

Rolf calls from the shore, "Last catch of the day, brother!"

The race is over. One of the boys who passed Erlann, raises his new sword.

Erlann looks at his reflection in the water and is at once confronted with the battered and bruised visage of himself. He's gutted; his arms are scraped up badly. Worse, he's lost another chance to win his sword. But Erlann's physical pain is nothing compared with the mental anguish of this latest failure. He rots on a rock as the crowd dissipates, judging himself as the water relentlessly passes by, like his latest opportunity—slipping away.

He looks up and sees Red and Rolf showing off each other's new swords as they walk on the other side of the river. A pack of smaller boys hangs on their every word as they commemorate their past success and foretell of future victories. Sven trails closely behind them, soaking up every word. Red points to Erlann across the river and seems to make a joke. Erlann cannot hear what they say, but Sven looks guiltily in his direction and laughs with the others as they walk away.

Then, Erlann is alone again.

Or perhaps not. The familiar sound of footsteps patter on the banks of the *Grenileir*. Erlann sees Axel's daughter, Loa, as she walks down to the water's edge. She holds her half of the amulet in one hand, its glow dissipating once again. Loa stands for a moment, looking out over the water. Reaching down, she picks up a pebble at her feet, and with a frustrated grunt, she hurls the pebble at the water. It lands with an inglorious plop as she reaches for another, and then another plop breaks the water.

Erlann softens. At least his misery will have some company this day. He quietly reaches down for a stone of his own. The flat stone zips past Loa's head as it skips across the water.

"A good toss," Loa remarks, making conversation.

She notices his wounds.

"You bleed."

Erlann's embarrassment is more than he can admit. "A *Brond Here* does not feel pain."

Erlann winces as he shifts his raw skin on the rock. He tries to hide this from Loa, but she sees. Mercifully, she plays along.

They go back to skipping stones.

Loa marvels, "We have no rivers like this in the wetlands."

She tosses another stone that plops flatly in the water.

Erlann instructs, "You'll get more use from the flat part of the stone."

Loa picks up another rock as Erlann demonstrates, saying, "Flick your wrist."

Loa observes the motion of his arm, and then she draws back, releasing a throw. The stone skips perfectly across the water. Loa jumps. She got it!

"Well done." Erlann picks up a comically big rock. "Time for a greater challenge."

He makes a big show of winding up his shoulders, and then, he just drops the rock. With no effort at all, it crashes through the surface of the river.

Sploosh!

This brings up a torrent of water, splashing Loa—who laughs!

Time passes quickly on the banks of the *Grenileir*. Loa and Erlann lie on the bank, resting, looking up at the sky. The light of the moons' eclipse gently illuminates the shore.

Loa whispers, "Where I am from, there are great lakes. The water is still, not like this *Grenileir*. After the winter snows, my brother and I would walk across. It was like a sheet of smooth glass. Then one day, he crossed to the far shore and did not come back."

Erlann breathes out heavily, admitting, "My mother passed when I was young. I will see her again someday in the *Halls of Iz*."

They look up at the moons.

"The brave live forever there, claimed by the spirit of *Baldr*. If that is true, my father and brother will surely be among that host someday."

Loa is touched. "Of all the reasons I have heard to take *The Trials*, that's the best, Erlann." Her hand moves close to his. "Your family will be reunited, in death if not in life."

Erlann turns to her. "What of your brother?"

Loa looks at her necklace. "My brother's half glows when my half is near. Given time, we will find him."

Their hands touch, and Erlann looks into Loa's eyes. She says gently, "Often I see him in my dreams."

Erlann leans in for a kiss, but as he does so, he catches a glimpse of Loa's half-necklace. Reflected in shadows between the fixtures and fastenings, he sees an image of Loa, her necklace is now complete but she's weeping uncontrollably as if all hope were lost.

Erlann pulls away as he spots Axel standing over them, seemingly from out of nowhere.

"Loa! There you are! Daughter, come," Axel snaps.

"Yes, father," replies Loa.

Axel glares at Loa. "Your brother would never have given up on you so easily."

Loa holds her necklace as she reports, "His trail grew cold outside the walls again."

"Then back to *Alstead* with you," Axel replies.

"I will find him, Father."

Loa turns to Erlann and says, "Thank you, Erlann, for showing me your trick with the stones."

Loa runs off. Erlann watches her go, but he soon looks back, as he feels Axel's cold, calculating eyes piercing into his half-naked body and through to his soul.

"Wars have been fought for less, boy. Keep your distance."

CHAPTER 12

THE BURDEN OF DECEIT

S PLASH! Salt water sprays up into the faces of the tired initiates. Their faces are grim and determined despite the freezing ocean spray. The crew of the boat, a sketchy lot, laughs from the dry, covered helm of the ship as they approach *Ey Sannhet*, the island of truth. Turning from the horizon, Erlann sees Sven shivering in the cold.

"Here," says Erlann.

He removes his cloak for Sven, who notices another boy looking over at them.

"I-I'm fine."

"For the cold, Sven," Erlann warmly insists.

"I said I'm fine!"

Sven moves away from Erlann, who is shocked by this change of behavior. Erlann finds himself alone again, standing in the chilly wind. He looks out into the dark horizon as a charred black island slowly floats into view. Through the fog and rain, Erlann sees no towns nor crops, no beast nor herbage, only a beautiful desolation of basalt and obsidian blanketing the surface with a fine pepper powder.

Standing on a black beach, Lady Strongbridge looks out over a volcanic landscape as the initiates disembark.

"Seven challenges have been met. Seven blades have been made. Two swords remain for the taking."

She turns and speaks in a disapproving tone. "Yet, two initiates possess swords already."

Rolf and Red lower their cowls. Erlann recognizes them as the remaining initiates gasp in shock. Rolf snarls at the crowd, "We will compete again."

Kare stomps his foot. "Outrageous!" The other boys grumble among themselves.

Marin speaks with more restraint, "Lady, there's no honor in this!"

Lady Strongbridge answers the initiates, "There's no rule barring their participation." She turns to Rolf and Red. "You would take another's destiny from them?" She probes. "Why?"

Rolf ignores the other initiates and gives his answer directly to Lady Strongbridge. "If any among these boys are true warriors . . ." Rolf stares down Erlann. "Then they have nothing to fear."

Lady Strongbridge gazes at Rolf and Red with *Brond* in her eyes. "Follow then."

As the group ascends the volcano, a cluster of parents follows closely behind. Reaching the summit and peering over the edge of a crater, the boys are taken aback by an unexpected sight—a dense bogland stretching as far as the eye can see. Lady Strongbridge speaks again.

"Of all virtues, *Truth* is the hardest to reach."

"More talk . . ." Rolf laughs and grabs at his crotch. "How do I claim my 'third' sword?"

Red laughs, as the other initiates glare at them silently.

Strongbridge points to the center of the crater in the far distance where a lonely tree stands. The crowd parts as the parents and onlookers make their way toward a rope bridge suspended from the crater's edge. It's carved into a platform in the far distance, an observation point in the sky.

Lady Strongbridge explains, "Brave the bog to the tree in the center. Pull the sword from the bark, and it's yours."

Red laughs. "True enough! Sounds easy."

Strongbridge looks to Erlann, and says, "I always speak true in this place."

Erlann considers the hidden meaning in her words.

"Well, come on, then!" Rolf waves. The initiates charge after Rolf making their way down into the bogland of the crater.

The initiates approach the edge of the bog with trepidation, their steps slowing as they gaze upon the desolate landscape stretching before them. Occasional pools of stagnant water mirror the rainy sky above, reflecting an almost endless somber gray.

"*Ey Sannhet*," Erlann says, speaking the name of this place.

Marin examines their path with apprehension. "There are stories from the sea. My father says there are monsters here."

Rolf turns and hisses, "Shut it."

Moving through melancholic mist, they venture further. The ground beneath their feet transforms into a soft, waterlogged earth, each step slightly sinking into a spongy surface. The bog hums with a symphony of raindrops as the mournful compression of unseen rot squishes underfoot. Each step brings a sense of impending doom. The land itself seems to hold memories of a bygone sorrow. The air hangs heavy with a palpable sadness, as if the very essence of the bog is in mourning. Erlann notices that the children are moving with a heaviness, as if this place were seeping into their souls. It's the weight of an unseen presence, hidden from perception, minding them from the shadows.

Marin watches the landscape. "*The Arema* once committed a great crime against the griffins and were cast into this bog by *Baldr* himself. To this day, they hide themselves." Marin continues, "So ashamed are they, that if anyone reminds them of their deed, they will pull them down into the murky dark, forever."

Time passes as the children slog through the muck. The silence of the bog weighs heavily, broken only by distant cries of unseen creatures and the sloshing of feet. Sparse vegetation, ghastly and forlorn, clings to life. The initiates observe twisted, gnarled shrubs that seem to weep, their branches reaching out like mournful arms.

As they navigate the treacherous bog, Erlann occasionally glances back, tracking the progress of the other initiates. He's surprised and somewhat delighted to see Sven engaging with other boys. Sven, normally an outcast among them, now appears to be charming the others with a wit previously unknown. Laughter and banter create a newfound camaraderie which somehow cuts through the gloom, clearing the way ahead.

There's solace in their collective unity as they march. However, Erlann's contentment begins to wane. Each time he looks back, the group seems to diminish, faces missing in the crowd, folks somehow disappearing into the shifting shadows of the bog. The laughter, once a source of joy, now takes on an eerie quality. A disquieting sensation settles over Erlann as he questions this change.

Torn between his desire for camaraderie and this unsettling realization, Erlann raises his guard. His initial joy gives way to a sense of foreboding as he grapples with the possibility that Sven's newfound charisma may be concealing something far more sinister.

"Erlann?" Sven calls out as he approaches from the shadows.

Erlann notices blood dripping from Sven's dagger that has been hastily returned to his belt.

Sven explains, "I've found a faster path to the tree. Follow me."

Suddenly, Sven sinks waist deep into the bog. Erlann reaches for Sven, but his hand slips awkwardly as they miss the connection.

"Marin!" Erlann yells.

Sven waves his arms, trying to grab onto anything he can. Erlann reaches out as far as possible, stretching his arms until they crack.

"Erlann! Erlann!" Sven yelps.

Marin runs to the other side of the pool and grabs Sven's hand. But it's too late. Whatever has Sven is pulling Marin down with him.

"Sven, forgive me. I can't . . ." She tries to let go, but Sven won't release her hand as they both sink deeper. "Sven!" Marin pleads for him to let her go.

But Sven grips her hand with a murderous stare as they descend into the muck.

"Sven. Release her!"

Suddenly, Kare lunges across, slicing through the middle of the two of them with his body, severing Sven's hold on Marin. The two land out of danger in an awkward position on the ground. Marin looks up at him.

"You have my thanks, Kare."

"Not bad, for a *Vein Clot*," Kare says softly.

Sven chokes on the dark water as he sinks down to his mouth. It seems he's beyond reach now. Sven, with terror in his eyes, tries to speak but only spits boggy muck. Between the gasps for breath and the strained choking, Erlann cannot understand him—as Sven's victims could not understand his actions, surely. Crushed, Erlann pushes himself closer to Sven. Though betrayed, he would hear the final words of this son of Northland.

"You'll not take my sword from me!"

Sven lashes out at Erlann with his dagger! Erlann dodges as Sven disappears below the surface, leaving only his shield floating quietly on the surface.

Erlann gasps, "These *Arema*? What was their crime?"

Marin speaks quietly, "They lied."

Erlann and Marin trade uneasy glances at the pool's edge. The initiates gaze downward, captivated by the bubbling mud concealing the sins and secrets of *Ey Sannhet*.

The troop resumes their journey, whispering quietly as they walk. Their progress through the bog is hampered by the greedy mud which gobbles each step they take. The haunting landscape seems to tighten its grip as, one by one, the children surrender to the relentless hunger of the mud, forever disappearing into the shadows cast by the twisted brush.

Despite all this, those who remain continue. The Tree, a lone sentinel in the heart of the bogland, beckons them. Its gnarled branches stretch toward the clouds casting a dark silhouette against the ever-present mist. The promise of the coveted prize whispered by Lady Strongbridge, acts as a siren's call, urging these pilgrims forward even as the bog claims them.

Then, Erlann sees it and exclaims, "The sword!"

Driven into the ancient bark of a solitary tree, the sword's blade glistens with a silver sheen—the runic symbol of *Truth* etched above its guard. It's like a silent watchman standing vigil through the gloom.

"It's there!" says Marin.

Erlann, Marin, Kare, Rolf, and Red dash for the tree. But the farther they run, the farther away it seems to be. No matter how quickly or how hard they try, it's out of reach. They stop in a huff, catching their breath.

Rolf jeers, "Keep up if you can!"

"You have your sword, pretender!" Erlann fires back.

Erlann dashes past Rolf, but they end up in exactly the same spot again—no closer to the tree. Erlann thinks, *What magic is this?*

"Magic or no, I'll reach that tree before any of you!" Rolf flexes and laughs to himself.

Red looks around nervously, uncharacteristically quiet for his disposition.

Erlann thinks for a moment and then speaks, "I always tell the truth in this place." He looks at Marin as she begins to understand.

"It's a clue," Marin states. "We might be lying to ourselves and counting something as ours we do not yet possess."

Erlann takes a moment and commands, "Clear your minds."

He closes his eyes, takes a deep breath, and takes a few steps forward. Opening his eyes, he measures the distance. It's closer than before.

"It's working!" Marin exclaims as she takes a step forward.

Rolf smiles at Erlann and quickly sprints after the sword. The chase is on! Marin slips and splashes into the bog, slamming her fist in anger. So clumsy! With a snide laugh, Red trips Erlann from behind. Leaving his feet, Erlann collides with Rolf, who in turn grabs Erlann as they both fall—this leads Red to trip in turn, sending Kare flying!

The initiates all spill into the mud. Splash!

Erlann's the first to leap up in the hustle for the tree. He looks over his shoulder and sees Rolf struggling to find his footing. Looking ahead, Erlann sees a clear path! He reaches the tree ahead of the others and tries to pull the sword out, but the tree will not yield its prize so easily. Bracing his foot against the trunk, he tries to rip the sword from the bark. Erlann hears his father's voice from above, which startles him.

"My son! Honor this day. From now till your end, you are known to *Baldr*."

Through the tangle of tree branches, Erlann sees an archaic observation post suspended above the bog. He sees Tyr raising his fists with joy as he watches from the platform above. A joyful cheer rings out from the lips of the spectators. It's a strange contrast in this somber place. As he approaches, Rolf is struck silent in this moment, studying his ill-gotten sword.

The bravado on his face transmutes to a sadness previously unknown to Erlann. Rolf wants to say something to his brother. Perhaps it's the truth.

"Brother . . ."

Suddenly, Rolf sinks!

"Rolf!" Erlann calls out to him as he tries even harder to draw the trapped sword from the tree.

"I didn't say anything! I didn't!" says Rolf, as panic fills his voice.

Red stands watching, as Rolf sinks up to his shoulders in mud.

Can silence lie? Erlann wonders.

Slurp! Red starts to sink.

"What?!!! Noooo!"

Erlann sees that the two are sinking at a fast rate.

"Rolf," Erlann scolds. "You have to tell Father the truth."

"About what?" Rolf says defiantly as he sinks to his chin.

"Rolf! You'll drown!"

"Then I drown a *Brond Here*," Rolf says stubbornly.

Red calls out, "Nonsense! Save me, Erlann!"

Rolf instructs Erlann, "Take both swords and leave me here." His eyes burn with stubbornness. "Do not dishonor me!"

Pinned to the tree, Erlann screams in frustration. He's furious with his brother's pride and his unwillingness to listen. But as his anger rises, a calmness washes over Rolf.

"It's alright. Let me go."

Erlann has to make a choice. He needs both hands to save the two boys. But if he lets go of the sword, his prize may be lost. Then Erlann realizes, if this is what it takes to be a *Brond Helm*, he does not want it.

"Fine. So be it."

Erlann abandons the sword in the tree and rushes to save the two boys! Rolf and Red are swiftly sinking as the crowd's collective gasps fill the air. Erlann plunges his arms deep into the muck, managing to pull both Rolf and Red onto the small island held together by the lonely tree. As they fall, Erlann sees a creature being pulled up out of the bog. It shrieks from a toothless mouth as it's pulled into the daylight. Almost frog-like, with a single closed eye it flops around, holding onto both Red and Rolf's legs.

Erlann calls to the *Arema*, "Be gone! Back to the muck with you!"

Unable to bear the daylight, it lets go and plunges back into the bog. Erlann catches his breath and then remembers, the sword! He turns to the tree but sees nothing but a hole in the trunk. It's gone.

"The sword of *Truth* has been claimed!" Lady Strongbridge announces from the observation post above.

Marin stands at the base of the tree, holding the sword up high.

Erlann has lost again. Rolf sneers at him as he pushes past, saying, "Watch yourself!" As the two boys make their way toward a rope ladder that's been dropped from the overhanging lookout post.

Erlann says nothing as Rolf and Red storm off, their stride tracked by Tyr, who regards Rolf with suspicion from the outpost.

"Erlann . . ." Marin glances at him apologetically.

He raises his hand stopping her. "Your sword has found you, Marin. A more honest person I have never known."

"You honor me," Marin says softly.

Erik, with a loud voice, shouts from the outpost above. "Where's Sven? Where is my son?"

The children do not answer. With a melancholy look, Kare holds up Sven's shield.

Back on the boat, Erlann and the other children huddle against the onslaught of squall and rain. They curl together behind Sven's warrior's shield, its once-gleaming surface now dulled by the same spray that stings their faces. The metal disc, too big for any one of their small arms to bear alone against the elements, rests heavy against their knees–a last piece of protection from the howling wind.

As the eastern shore of Northland breaks through the mist, Erlann spots *Brond Helm* Erik wandering the deck of the ship. Soaked to the bone with despair, he lashes upon the moons and sky with his voice, feeling swindled by the things that are.

"*Baldr*! Where have you taken my boy? Come down here, coward, and give him back to me! Sven!!!! Sven!!!!!!"

As merciless sea salt stings his eyes; Erlann thinks, *"All the rivers and all the seas could not fill the emptiness left by this terrible day."*

The angry sea mirrors Erik's grief as he rages toward the sky. No one dares to say anything, yet somehow he laments for all the initiates who have died in these trials, those countless souls lost in the spans of time, as the ship bears to shore.

The sound of rain patters on the cobblestones outside the windows of *Stalden Keep*. Erlann, having safely returned from the day's events—sits on his bed listening to the rainfall. There's almost no wind, but a quiet stillness like a waterfall raining from the sky.

Tyr enters. He quietly haunts the doorway trying to find words of comfort; failing this, he sits down next to Erlann putting his arm around his son's shoulder.

Then, it all bursts out, the stress of the past few days. Erlann sobs uncontrollably, burying his head in Tyr's arm. Tyr sits quietly, his hand on Erlann's shoulder as the rain quietly falls.

CHAPTER 13

SHADOW WALKERS

E rlann awakens to the sound of footsteps in the hall. It's still dark
outside, yet the rain has stopped.

Pretty late for a visitor, he thinks, as a shadowy figure enters his room.
An assassin? Could it be? Erlann reaches underneath his straw pillow for his
dagger. Gripping it tightly, he lies still, waiting. Just as the intruder's hand
reaches down and touches his shoulder he flips over, preparing to strike!
But he calms when he sees the cloaked visage of Elda floating over him.

"Grandmother," Erlann whispers, on the verge of tears. "Did you
know how many would die?"

Elda considers his words for a brief moment. "Death is the price of
life. Sooner or later, we all pay the toll."

Erlann responds with words that harbor more of an accusation than a
question. "Did you know what price Sven was willing to pay?"

"Come," Elda replies softly.

Erlann rises from his bed and follows Elda out of the room.

The banks of the *Grenileir River* shine in the moonlight. This time of the
span, the sun never truly sets; it simply hangs in twilight low on the horizon. Erlann knows this place where they walk. It's *Stanheng Hol,* an ancient
temple ringed with sandstone hedges. It's said that the first folk crawled

from the clay in this very place by the river's edge. Its sacred stones line the exterior of the compound, a silent record of the history and law of Northland. No one, not even Thane, would violate the sanctity of this holy place without devastating consequences.

Elda walks toward the temple and says, "There are places where the veil of this world is thin."

"Grandmother?" Erlann ponders her words but does not understand.

"I am no deranged fortune teller, asking questions of the stars. Tonight we will walk in the shade between life and death," Elda says cryptically. "Between the present and all of experience."

"The Great In-Between." Erlann understands. "Is it evil?"

"No more evil than the rain watering crops, or a flood washing away a township. It's the mountain that burns, or the sun that warms. It's part of the nature of being."

They enter the main temple and descend a set of old venerable steps into an open room. The chamber has a channel cut into its ceiling which aligns with the light of the moon. This beam illuminates a narrow path from the staircase to an altar carved from the bedrock.

"It lies in the shadows all around us," Elda says with a tone of awe, "waiting to be known."

Erlann follows Elda to the altar and watches as she carefully pulls down on a lever in the center. To his surprise, water rushes into the chamber, flooding its lower depths, leaving only the walkway unsubmerged. This path is little more than a catwalk suspended by chains of *brond*.

Elda turns. "There are words closer to the heart of creation, and water can be used to conduct the path."

Erlann looks apprehensively toward the end of the walkway. "What's in there?"

There's a warning in Elda's words. "What you bring is what you find."

Erlann strains his eyes, peering into the dark shadows at the end of the path. Elda watches him with equal parts concern and excitement. She closes her eyes and speaks the *shadow words* for the first time in Erlann's presence:

"Se flód tíma is hweorfa."

Elda repeats the words over and over in a light whisper, motioning for Erlann to repeat them. As he does so, the shadows around the chamber grow darker somehow, but the path remains well-lit by moonlight.

"*Se flód tíma is hweorfa.*"

"Walk the path. Go!" Elda instructs with haste.

Erlann repeats the words as he walks toward the shadows at the end of the walkway. As he approaches, through the darkness he makes out a shape of something standing in place. It stands very still, at the end of the path.

It's waiting for me, he thinks. *Is it a trick?* Erlann studies the surroundings, but there are no windows or trap doors from which this figure could have emerged. He looks back toward his grandmother, and in that moment, he knows she sees it too. She bids him to continue with a silent nod. Erlann summons all his courage, forcing his focus on the mechanical exercise of placing one foot after the other. Erlann comes very close to the figure now; he looks up from his boots as the shadowy silhouette moves soundlessly toward him.

What's this? Erlann thinks to himself.

Erlann watches as the mysterious figure steps into the moonlight. His breath catches as he recognizes himself—older, crowned, and radiating an air of regal authority. It's as if this figure has stepped directly out of his previous vision, the one reflected in the puddle of blood. Across the way, the warrior locks eyes with him, standing at the end of the path.

The entity—his future self—seems as real as Erlann or his grandmother. Yet, its nature remains a mystery to him: a consciousness born of the Great In-Between. Erlann halts a few paces away, cautious and uneasy. This is no mere reflection or fleeting vision; it feels undeniably alive. Instinct warns him to tread carefully, to weigh his words with precision.

Then, surprisingly, the crowned apparition smiles in greeting, and says, "If you could undertake one thing, one venture, and neither falter nor fail, what would you choose?"

"I wish to take my place as a *Brond Here*."

The apparition stares at him with no reaction.

Erlann searches deeper, looking further into himself. After a time, he speaks again.

"The harder I try, though, to control my destiny, the more I will try to dominate my brethren."

The apparition bears an accepting smile and reaches for Erlann, who is no longer afraid as he pulls in closer to his older self. The younger merges with the older, as Erlann melts into mist and shadow. He passes through the older aspect of himself toward the end of the path. What was once a dead end is now a bright hallway of pure light, its power cutting through the shadows.

Erlann turns back and sees Elda, standing still as a stone. Time has once again slowed. He's alone; there's but one course now. Breathing in deeply, he steps forward to walk in this path of light. As he proceeds, he hears muffled voices ahead. With every step, the murmur of a crowd becomes clearer as the light of the hall grows brighter. It's a whirl of incantations mixed with the quiet cries of weeping and despair. He's close now. The light pours in, blinding him, and forcing him to close his eyes in pain. But as he does so, this assault of light and sound collapses into the dark of silence.

All is still.

Erlann stands in place, listening, as a gentle chant rises from the quiet. He recognizes the sacred words of the *Daughter's of Freya*. They have many words. Words of solidarity. Words of loneliness. Words for the war-weary and the purification of blood guilt. Words for the loss of a child. Words to celebrate those who have gone to *Baldr's* side on the moon of *Iz*, and words to comfort those who will not.

As they sing a song of release, the lyrics speak of letting go. Their chant laments for those still living, having been left behind by the departing dead as those souls journey into the Great In-Between. In his mind, Erlann reasons, as *a cup of water poured out cannot fill a lake, so too will the mind, body, and spirit dissipate into the void*. Erlann winces, knowing this ritual is all too common for the families of Northland.

After a moment, Erlann carefully opens his eyes and sees *Bálstaðr*, the burning place, nestled on the far side of the *Grenileir*, opposite the temple. As the son of a *Brond Helm*, Erlann knows it well. The fire ceremony is for *The Brond* alone. Many ritual hearths line the river bank as if assembled into battle formation. They serve a dual purpose for a *Brond* who falls on the field of justice: first to free the spirit from the body, and then to light their journey through the Great In-Between, to the *Halls of Iz*—where the just live forever.

In the center of the grounds, a funeral commences with all the trappings and pomp fit for a queen. Erlann steps forward with a creeping dread in his heart as he tries to catch a closer look. But it's not Elda laying on the pile of kindling; it's Erlann's mother. A young, beautiful woman, she lays in pale contrast to the platform of ribbons, sticks, and logs. Dressed in a gown of white, she's surrounded by the food and provisions needed for her journey. Then, Erlann catches sight of his own reflection in the water. He sees himself at the age of five, looking back at him from the river. Erlann realizes these are not future days, but the past, long set, from many spans ago. In fact, he notices he was standing in this very spot on this very day as a young boy.

He sees his father, Tyr, approaching the platform—leaning over Erlann's mother in a quiet, tearful farewell.

A consoling hand rests on Erlann's shoulder.

It's Rolf at seven spans of age. "Brother. What has happened this day?"

"Mother." Erlann turns, speaking in place of his younger self, "She has fallen on the mountaintop."

Rolf's voice has a shade of warning, "She died bravely then."

"Yes."

"One day, I will take the trails." Rolf beams. "Complete what Mother began, in her name."

Erlann proclaims, "Rolf, Mother's trial wasn't finished. Why has she been taken to the burning place?"

Rolf gives Erlann a hard look.

Silence fills the space between them.

Just then, Elda, ten spans younger, emerges from the darkness with a crown fixed to her hair. A hush comes over the assembled crowd as they wait to hear her speak. She carries a lit torch, looking out into a sea of faces. For a moment, it seems she might speak. But instead, she tosses the burning torch onto the pyre. Soon, the kindling blazes with the brightness of the fire moon itself.

"My warriors. Friends. Kin." She looks directly at Erlann and then resumes the speech. "We have fought many battles. Shared many dangers."

Elda turns back toward the group. "Tonight, it has become clear to me that I can no longer serve *Baldr's* will and remain your queen."

The crowd erupts with shock and confusion. They protest her words, but Erlann has never seen his grandmother back down once a decision has been made.

"Silence! This is my final command to you." Elda raises her hands to her head, gripping the crown. "Henceforth, all those who have shown their quality, all the *Brond* of Northland, will speak their own mind and hold fast to it!"

She hurls the crown into the roaring flames of her daughter's funeral pyre, to the gasps of all. Then, as suddenly as this scene materialized, it recedes, disappearing into the shadow and mist once again. Erlann is left alone, next to the burning pyre of his mother.

He approaches the funeral hearth. Peering through the flames, he sees the ashen remains of his mother disintegrating in the heat. Erlann stops. Above her, on her chest, glittering in the flicker, sits the golden crown of the once-queen. He's very close to the fire; he should feel heat. But he does not. Slowly, carefully, he raises his hand. After a moment of brief testing, he reaches into the flames. But he's not burned. An illusion, it seems. Taking a moment to reflect on his mother's fate, he picks up the crown, pulling it from the flames.

The firelight recedes. Erlann finds himself back in the ancient temple with Elda. He still holds the crown in his hands, taken from the Great In-Between.

"What's this? I've not seen this," Elda gasps.

An empty chair appears through the shadows before Erlann. He recognizes it as Elda's throne from the catacombs. He places the crown on the seat as it melts back into the dark. He turns to Elda, who is at a loss for words.

The future has changed somehow, Erlann thinks, feeling it in his heart. Could it be he will avoid this bloody fate after all, and live out his days in peace? Erlann has nothing but questions as Elda approaches on the walkway.

"Erlann, well done!"

Erlann has never heard such excitement or hope, in her voice.

She stares and him and says, "We must brave deeper now. I must go farther into the Great In-Between. Everything is realigning. We must discover a better fate for our people."

"Shall I go with you, Grandmother?"

"No! No, my sweet boy. You've done well enough this night, but you have much to learn before you walk the shadows of the Great In-Between."

Erlann nods, confident his lack of knowledge would only be a hindrance at this time. He must study more about the Great In-Between.

Elda puts her hand on his cheek.

"The hour is late, Erlann." Elda speaks gently. "Rest and restore your bones."

With a gleam in her eye, she backs away from him and into the dark, disappearing into the shadows. Erlann stands alone again, with only the crickets of the riverbank to keep him company. With a long sigh, he turns and begins the long and lonely walk back to *Alstead*.

CHAPTER 14

THE COST OF PRIDE

I t's dawn, and Erlann sits alone in the courtyard of *Stalden Keep*. His feet rest on the steps leading down to the mead cellar, a quieter part of the complex. His gaze is drawn to the clashing of wooden swords, as a group of younger boys practice their fight-craft. Suddenly, Rolf and Red leap from the crowd, brandishing their real swords. The boys cheer Rolf on as he fights with Red.

They spar roughly, drawing a small crowd. Red slashes at Rolf's forearm, causing a nick.

"Gah!" As Rolf reacts to the pain, Red swiftly disarms him in an unexpected move.

Rolf laughs. "Go again! You boys wish to be ready?" Rolf sticks out his chest. "Watch this."

Erlann sits, observing in disgust, as the two boys launch into yet another duel.

"Well met, Erlann," says a strong, gravelly voice.

Erlann turns to see Thane's Herald, who has emerged from the cellar door sipping a cup of mead. He's never been this close to a *Stafntaki* before, and this is quite close enough. There's a dark cunning about them, a cruelty always ready to spring when weakness presents itself.

Animals, Erlann thinks to himself.

"Preparing for the final trial, are we?" Egil makes conversation with a sly tone of voice as he creeps up the stairs.

Erlann hits him with a sidelong glance as Egil sits across from him. They sit in silence watching the other boys spar in the courtyard. Rolf pins Red's sword to the ground and kicks it, disarming him. Kare returns Red's sword to him from the ground with a spry laugh. The crowd chooses sides, chanting in favor of either Rolf or Red.

Herald Egil continues, "I've witnessed you in *The Trials*. You deserve victory, yet it keeps slipping away."

"My time will come," Erlann responds quietly.

"For your sword." Herald Egil nods. "Yes, indeed. At my *Gathering*, I would have done anything to win my sword."

Erlann doesn't like where this is going, and he demands, "Speak your purpose."

The herald reveals a sword under his dark cloak.

"Why trust your future to chance? The return of the king is nigh, and King Thane will be most generous to those who accept his lordship."

Egil offers his sword; Erlann is tempted for a moment but shakes the thought from his mind.

"Keep your sword, Herald; it has no sweat on the grip."

Egil smiles as a voice interrupts from behind.

"Do you have my brother under your cloak as well?"

Erlann turns and sees Loa standing with her father, Axel. Her tired red eyes betray the determination of her voice. She has not slept since arriving in Alstead, but bears her charge with quiet determination and undiminished charm.

Axel's voice fills with hostility, "Be gone snake, and take your little fang with you."

Erlann can detect something of a smirk beneath the cowl of Egil's hood.

"As you wish," Egil says as he slithers away.

Axel probes Erlann's face with his piercing eyes as Loa looks at her dimming amulet in despair. "You do not train as the others do?"

"I shall take the next *Gathering*, my part in these trials are finished," Erlann says flatly.

Loa stares at Erlann with confusion in her eyes.

Erlann explains himself, "The last trial is a battle circle; one final fight to the last man standing. I will not draw my brother's blood."

Rolf disarms Red once more, sending his sword soaring through the air. The boys erupt in cheers as Rolf triumphantly lifts his arms in celebration. Red's sword flops to the ground near Erlann's feet; this incites an awkward pause. In a huff, Red approaches Erlann.

"Some aid, good *Brond*," Red commands with mock courtesy.

Erlann glares back. "You know I am forbidden to hold a sword."

As they appear to be in a standoff, a crowd surrounds them.

"Pick it up, dog!" snarls Red.

Axel unsheathes his sword, offering the hilt to Erlann. "In matters of insult, I have never cared much for rules."

Erlann smiles at Loa. "A *Brond Here* does not need a weapon." He pivots to Red with a sneer on his lips. "A *Brond Here* is a weapon!"

Red reaches back for a punch, but not before Erlann rises with a head-butt—decking Red square in the nose. The force sends him staggering backward.

Kare's eyes grow as big as saucers.

"FIGHT!!!!!" the crowd joins in shouting as Kare hollers with fists raised.

Erlann and Red grapple in the dust. The shouting faces of boys are seen in the sky above as they roll around on the ground. Erlann gets the better of Red, vaulting on top. He beats him with strike after strike.

"Hold!" Rolf screams, as he tries to break up the fight, pulling the boys apart. "Hold!" He grabs Erlann by the armpits. "Erlann, ho-!"

Erlann's furious. He pulls his fist back for another strike, but instead rams his elbow into Rolf's eye. All grows silent as Rolf staggers back from Erlann. A flash of terror overtakes Erlann as he fears that he may have taken out his brother's eye. Rolf blinks once, then twice. A sudden look of indignation washes over Rolf's face and he draws his real sword.

"Rolf!" Erlann warns.

"Guard yourself."

Rolf's swing cuts through the air toward Erlann. With a swift dodge, Erlann pulls Axel's sword from its sheath and parries a follow-up strike from Rolf. The two brothers exchange determined glares as the sound of *Brond* grinds against itself. In a sudden move, Rolf kicks Erlann in the shin, toppling him onto his back.

Rolf roars, "This time you stay down."

Rolf's sword arcs swiftly toward Erlann. Erlann reacts with precision, deflecting the blade into the ground and twisting his own sword in a single fluid motion. As Rolf stumbles forward, Erlann's blade finds its mark, pressing against his brother's neck. In the same instant, Rolf's sword brushes against Erlann's throat, each drawing a thin line of blood. The crowd gasps as the brothers freeze, their killing blows halted in perfect synchrony.

The wound is shallow. A slender stream of Rolf's blood trickles down the blade. Erlann pivots, catching Rolf's dark reflection in the polished steel. Time slows as a sequence of movements unfold in the mirrored surface. Erlann shuts his eyes, rejecting this gift of foresight, this unwelcome reflex. No! He won't see, not this time!

Rolf bellows and strikes again, too swift for Erlann to counter as the world snaps back to normal speed. A powerful punch lands, forcing the breath from Erlann's lungs. He staggers, gasping for breath as he's thrown backward, his sword clattering to the ground.

Seizing the advantage, Rolf hacks at an unarmed Erlann ferociously. Erlann strains to dodge the quick blows, concentrating on Rolf as he weaves in and out. Enraged, Rolf brings the blade down for a killing stroke. But Erlann catches the hilt with his hand.

"Rolf! Stop this!" Erlann pleads.

The two boys struggle for control of the sword.

"ENOUGH!!!!" A gruff voice booms through the courtyard.

Tyr's bear-sized hand reaches in, hoisting Rolf off his feet and hurling him back a safe distance away. Erlann turns to find Loa on the steps, hands clasped to her mouth in horror. Rolf smirks, noticing Erlann now holds a sword in their father's presence. Realizing this, Erlann recoils in shame.

Rolf speaks with a smug expression on his face, "He holds a sword, Father!"

Erlann releases the sword as a disappointing clang rings loudly on the ground.

Tyr ignores Rolf, "Back. All of you."

The boys back away.

Rolf speaks again, "Fathe—" Tyr raps his mouth with the back of his hand.

Tyr hunches over him, menacingly.

"This family does not spill its own blood."

Erlann knows this has gone too far. "It was a brother's fight, Father. Forgive us."

Rolf sneers, "What brother have I?! One who holds no confidence!"

Erlann doesn't understand.

Tyr jams his finger in Rolf's face, "Silence! On your life!"

Rolf slaps Tyr's hand out of the way and stares him down with a look of defiance, "Save your breath for one who respects it."

Tyr swings at him again, but this time Rolf catches Tyr's hand in his own. Rolf holds Tyr's palm defiantly, showing his full strength.

Tyr smiles grimly, taunting him, "So, you're a *Brond Here* now, are you? Won the sword of *Fidelity*, did you?"

Tyr reaches into the pouch on his belt and produces a griffon's egg— Rolf's egg from the Trial of *Fidelity*. Rolf freezes. There's nothing he can say. Their father knows the extent of his terrible secret. A cracking sound is heard as Tyr breaks the egg with a closed fist.

"This is no more a griffon's egg than a shithouse is a mead hall!"

Rolf has been had but dares not give an inch.

Tyr leans in, so the others cannot hear. "Do you know what the penalty is for pretenders?"

Tyr grabs Rolf with both arms and shoves him against the wall. Rolf tries to resist, but Tyr has him pinned.

"Be still!"

Tyr draws his dagger; its serrated edges are sharp, gleaming in the light.

"First, I take my dagger, son, and I saw into your back, as the woodsmen cut the forest."

Tyr's blade slides down the surface of Rolf's shirt.

"Second, I peel your ribs back, boy, as the cook serves oysters from the sea. Then, I pull your breath from you, take it from your back, and as two mead sacks, they hang . . . leaving you wheezing for air. As you draw your last breath, pretender, you'll know you will never see the Halls of *Iz*. This justice, this Bloody Griffon, only a *Brond Helm* can deliver."

Tyr lets Rolf fall to the ground as he sheaths his dagger.

Red collects him from the cobblestones. "Rolf! Let's go," he whispers.

Rolf turns to go without saying a word as Kare and several other boys follow them out quietly.

Axel gathers his sword from the ground and re-sheathes it. "No way to treat a sword, boys," he remarks.

CHAPTER 15

TWILIGHT OF HOPE

E rlann follows closely behind his father, Tyr, and Axel. They ascend the well-trodden steps leading up to the top of a parapet—one of many defensive towers that ring the keep. The usual watchmen have been reinforced by additional guards, their armor glistens dramatically under the dim light of the eclipsed moons. The guards are alert, vigilant, and prepared: not for *The Trials*, but for the looming threat of the coming prisoner exchange with the pretender Thane.

As they reach the highest point of *Stalden Keep*, a view unfolds before them—the great city of *Alstead* with its many tiered levels. This sprawling place, usually bustling with individual activity, now seems like a single entity as folks line the streets for the coming celebration. The roads are adorned with thistles, and the people gather with bouquets, eagerly awaiting the return of their kin with joy and anticipation.

Yet the heightened security is palpable, with guards stationed at critical points in the city, standing in silent observation. They exchange vigilant glances as Tyr surveys the surroundings. His gaze is unwavering, and Erlann senses the urgency as he studies every detail of the defense. Axel is present as well, double-checking the deployment of his own men. The two *Brond Helms* look down on *Alstead*, assessing their readiness.

"There's been no word from the outer pickets," Tyr relays.

"It matters not. I'll ready the prisoners," replies Axel.

Tyr raises his hand. "Hold. Let Thane's men sit in chains a little longer."

His gaze returns to the people below, gathering for the celebration.

"Worry not. Even Thane would not make war during *The Gathering*," Axel says, with concern.

Tyr smiles with scorn. "No one would. That's what worries me."

Axel drops all pretense of courtesy. "Thane's an animal. But to risk True Death during the eclipse? *Baldr* cannot see from the *Halls of Iz* as long as the fires of *Brond* block his view. That would mean eternal death for anyone who falls in battle."

A horn blows. "Wagons! South face!" a sentry shouts.

Axel sighs, "Long have we waited for this moment." He exclaims, "Loa! Your brother, today is his release!"

"I'll go and bring him, Father!" Loa exclaims, smiling as she runs off.

Tyr commands, "Guard! Go tell the *Brond Voldur* that the hostages have arrived."

Axel nods. "I've prepared my own guard as well. If this is a trap, it will be King Thane's last."

Tyr nods as Erlann ventures closer to his father, though ashamed, he still wishes to help.

"Father? What can I do?"

Tyr rests his hand on Erlann's shoulder. "It's for the *Brond* to 'do,' son."

More reinforcements come. As the *Brond Voldur* march by the group in full regalia, their sheer formidability seems to mock Erlann's offer of aid with every footstep. What could a boy like him do to help the *Brond*? Erlann understands the most he can strive for this day is to stay out of the way, as he hikes back toward the keep.

Rolf walks through the markets of *Alstead* with Red, Kare, and their remaining group of sparring mates. The crowd is packing in along the roadside, with their thistles, tassels, and other celebratory trinkets. With each step, Rolf feels something unexpected—more flushed and weaker. It's almost as if his sullen heart were driving this sickness.

"Rolf! I will win *The Honor Circle* tonight. I can feel it," Kare exclaims, jumping with excitement.

Rolf doesn't answer; his breathing grows heavier with each attempt. The wound on his neck bubbles, turning black, as bile runs down from a gaping sore.

"Rolf, are you well?" one of the boys asks.

Red smirks. "Are you his mother, boy?"

Rolf fights through the pain as the boys look to the road, trying to find a space in the gathering crowd,

"I can't see the wagons," another boy exclaims straining to gain a view of the festivities. "Can't see anything with these folks in the way!"

"Take to the walls, then!" Red suggests.

Rolf forces bravado through his increasing exhaustion. "Let's go!"

The boys race for the tower at the wall's edge.

Red beckons them to a door nestled in the stone. "This way!"

Rolf stops, catching his breath. He's very dizzy but tries to fight through it. "A moment."

"Almost there!" answers Red.

Rolf digs for strength and follows Red into the tower.

"We'll miss the exchange! Hurry!" another boy says.

They climb the steps on the inside wall of the tower as the crowd outside cheers. Rolf throws open the hatch at the top of the stairs and climbs through the floor into the guard tower. The shutters of the room are closed, keeping the outside light at bay; save for a few stray beams that slip through the cracks.

The children struggle to find their way as they adjust to the pitch.

"It's so dark," Kare says.

Rolf appears to be having real trouble now, as he leans against the wall.

"Bring a light," says another boy.

Rolf looks around. "Where's Red?"

"What's this?" Rolf says out loud as another dizzy spell hits him. Just about to fall, he grabs hold of an armament table to steady himself. As he holds on, his hand squishes into a liquid that's dripping from the table to the floor. Rolf looks at his fingers. They're covered in blood, recently shed. He looks around the room as his eyes adjust.

He sees five guards; all have been killed quietly without alarming the wider garrison. In the corner, among the bodies, Red squats in a beam of light. His face has the look of a successful prank pulled.

"There are monsters in the burning south. Even if you strike them down, their gore will vex you."

Rolf touches the side of his neck where earlier, Erlann's sword had gashed him. Red mirrors him with mock discomfort as Rolf realizes what has happened. He winces as the festering wound throbs with a sickly heat. The poisoned gash oozes black, bubbling bile, revealing the insidious nature of the poison.

"Oh. This is not your brother's fault. I'm quite surprised his patience held as long as it did. You never recognized me? I blame you not. We were all so young when our families broke apart. How sad that after all these spans, you know not your cousin's face."

A look of horror washes over Rolf. It's Thane's son.

Marauder, killer, the personification of vengeance in his father's name. His mission: to make the people of Northland pay for their disloyalty through sack and ransom. If they will not tithe to their king, they will pay through blood. Or worse still, to be pressed into the service of the pretender, which would be a terror worse than death. Stolen folks are tortured, broken, and then reborn through pain into the ranks of the *Stafntaki*.

Fear is not a feeling Rolf has ever truly been acquainted with, but it does have a name. "Geir!" Rolf rasps.

He tries to draw his sword as his strength leaves him. Geir listens as another cheer comes from the outside.

"Fear not, cousin. My father would have you live, for now." Geir gives him a mischievous look. "About the fate of others, my father remained silent."

The boys are attacked and overwhelmed by Thane's men, who pour out of the shadows in unknown numbers. They're badly outmatched. As the boys go down, Kare lunges at the nearest of Thane's men. He strikes him across the head with Sven's shield, killing him instantly.

"Rolf! Run!" Kare calls out with desperation.

Losing his balance, Rolf sinks to the floor and tries to crawl to safety. The remaining boys die in the dark, cut down by a flurry of blades. Kare fights valiantly but is overwhelmed by these terrible enemies. He's stabbed from behind, the last to fall.

Losing consciousness, Rolf's vision blurs as all his remaining strength fails.

Geir pushes his finger into the wound on Kare's back who now lays prostrate on the floor. This causes the boy to wince in pain.

"With hunger, as the wolf, I devour my prey."

Thane's men respond in a religious tone, ". . . as all will be devoured."

Rolf's eyelids flutter as he rolls in and out of consciousness. He sees Kare has been mortally wounded. Trying to comfort him, Rolf reaches for Kare with an outstretched hand. Tears fill Kare's eyes as he realizes that, for him, there will be no life beyond his death.

"I see no light . . . no hall. I see nothing."

Kare's pupils dilate, revealing an all-too-familiar stare into nothingness. He's fallen into True Death. Rolf cannot hold his eyes open any longer; the poison takes its full effect as his consciousness dissolves.

He feels the *Stafntaki* scoop him up by his arms and legs as they bear him down the stairs. Rolf's assaulted by light and sound as he and his captors exit the tower by the roadside. With a deep, heavy thump, he looks up as the gates of *Alstead* open. Thane's wagons enter the city to the elation of a cheering crowd. Rolf's gut tightens in dread as he hears their unbridled joy. It's the sound of anticipation, of the sons of Northland being returned to their mothers, daughters, and wives. The voices of a stolen generation so close to being made whole.

The first wagon passes through the doors of *Alstead*. It's the grandest of all, perhaps the greatest Rolf has seen in his short life. The dark carriage adorned with red velvet curtains and black-gold trim, is led by a team of large muscular horses. As it passes by, the back door swings open before Rolf who is unceremoniously tossed inside.

A powerful voice is heard. Though quiet in tone, its timbre is piercing and passes through Rolf with every word.

"You have done well, Prince Geir."

Rolf looks up toward the voice. There's a giant figure illuminated through the curtains, though only partially. The figure leans forward on his seat. It's Thane, a giant bear-head helm adorning his brow. "Today is our homecoming."

Thane holds out a vial of Fenreir's blood.

Geir drinks to their inevitable triumph.

"Welcome home, Father, my King."

He passes the vial to other *Stafntaki* in the wagon, who all partake in this rite. It's almost time, Thane leans back as he waits patiently.

The man who would be king glares at the joyful crowd through crimson curtains.

Geir cannot contain his excitement as he exits the cabin. He vaults up next to the driver of the lead wagon and surveys the scene. Hyah! The entire city celebrates as dozens of wagons roll up the street toward the inner walls of *Stalden Keep*.

Thistles rain down on the convoy from the upper levels as they pass.

All smiles, Loa pushes her way to the front of the crowd preparing to toss a thistle. She's just in time to spot Geir sitting in the driver's box. As he rides by, he turns and gives her a wink. In this moment of recognition, Loa drops her thistle onto the muddy road. Her good spirits are crushed as the churn of heavy wagon wheels rip the petals asunder. Loa knows that if Geir rides with Thane's men, it can only mean one thing: treachery. Armed with the knowledge of this betrayal, she heads for the keep. But throngs of ecstatic people block her path. She becomes more and more desperate as she pushes upstream into a sea of smiles.

Erlann sits on the keep wall, wallowing in guilt. "Erlann! ERLANN!" Loa tries to get his attention from below, but Erlann does not hear. Her voice is drowned out by the crowd as he sulks on the parapet.

The lead wagon rolls to the inner gate that separates *Stalden Keep* from the city below. Geir announces the wagon train from high up on his seat. "Hail! To the people of *Alstead*. We bring great tidings from your king."

The Sentry, unimpressed, raises his arm to begin his inspection. "Hold."

Geir jumps down from the wagon and smiles as he lands on the ground. "Of course, perform your office." He leans in. "Do you like your office? My driver does. I do too. I love my office, actually. So many people sleepwalk through life."

The sentry approaches the wagon for a closer inspection. Seeing a figure in the window, the guard ventures in for a closer look.

Geir growls, "I, however, have never felt more alive."

Suddenly, The sentry realizes that Rolf, The *Bond Helm's* son is propped against the window, beaten and unconscious.

The Sentry calls, "To arms!"

Geir runs the sentry through with his sword of *Industriousness*, savoring the moment. He drinks in the experience, watching the guard bleed out on the ground. With a loud crack, Thane breaks through the top of the lead wagon, splitting it apart from the inside out.

"Now, my warriors, strike now!"

Thane's warriors pour out of their wagons in overwhelming numbers. Dressed in wolf hides and leather armor, they form their ranks, preparing to attack. The sentries, paralyzed with confusion, raise their daggers and spears, but they're at a gross disadvantage without swords. Violence of any kind is not allowed during the eclipse, and yet it has come to their doorstep.

Thane vaults from the wagon and rushes for *Stalden* gate as Geir removes the guards of the lower gatehouse from Thane's path with a series of well-placed axe throws.

From up high, a sentry calls, "Drop the gate!"

Thane raises the vial necklace to his lips, taking a deep gulp of Fenreir's blood. Everyone watches in terror as this behemoth of a man somehow grows even larger.

He lunges for the closing drop gate, jamming his war hammer between it and the ground. The guards from inside the keep watch in horror as Thane single-handedly raises the gate with his newfound strength.

"Fear the one, TRUE, KING!"

Several of Thane's men rush past him, ducking under the gate to press their advantage into the courtyard. Trumpets sound as the *Brond Voldur* rush in to meet this incursion with brave minds and stout hearts. The call of battle rings in the keep as the sounds of metal and death fill the air.

CHAPTER 16

A HOUSE DIVIDED

Back on the parapet, Erlann sits alone. Suddenly, there's a huge burst of activity as a host of *Voldur* run by. Erlann leaps to his feet and runs after them.

"What's this? What's happened?"

"We are betrayed!" A *Brond* proclaims.

At the main gate, strips of wood are being stacked under the portcullis, where a crude wedge is being constructed. Thane holds the drop gate aloft with inhuman strength as his men inside the courtyard sacrifice themselves to protect him.

Geir barks orders to the *Stafntaki* as they finish construction, "Hurry, you dogs!"

A *Stafntaki* places the last plank of wood, but it's not quite high enough to support Thane's shoulders. They're still a little short. Geir eyes a quick solution. He squares up and strikes the trooper in the back with his throwing axe, killing him. The body falls perfectly into place on the pile. Thane, hands freed, lowers his arms and steps over the threshold into the main yard of *Stalden Keep*. Their attack goes from a trickle to a flood as Thane's men pour unimpeded through the main gate of Stalden

Keep. The courtyard explodes in a desperate pitched battle. But without swords, the *Brond* are being cut down by the advancing *Stafntaki*.

"The inner gate is lost!" a guard shouts as he rushes by.

He sprints fast through the courtyard with panic in his eyes. Erlann chases him to the main wooden doors of *Stalden Keep*. Out of breath, he raises his hand in mid-stride, "Hold the doors! Wait!"

The guard doesn't notice Erlann behind him and slams the door directly in his face. Erlann's locked out! He pounds on the door, but no matter how hard he screams, it doesn't open. He then feels a set of eyes burning into his back as he looks behind him. Thane walks relentlessly through the maelstrom of battle toward Erlann and the door.

Then, one of the metal-reinforced portholes along the side of the keep unlocks and opens. Lady Strongbridge peeks out through the opening.

"Son of Tyr!"

Strongbridge pulls Erlann through the portal into her chambers as a flurry of arrows flies by. One of Strongbridge's attendants slams the portal window shut and relocks it. Erlann looks up at him from the floor and sees that this 'servant of the mountain' is armed to the teeth—with hammer and shield.

"Your man is no servant," Erlann says.

"He serves *Stor Doren*, as do I," responds Lady Strongbridge cryptically. Her servants, fitted with full battle armor cover all possible entrances, listening for any breach or intrusion.

Erlann leans in and pleads, "Ambassador, you must help us."

Strongbridge speaks with a diplomatic tone, "With axe and armor, blood and tears, no. This we are forbidden."

Erlann's heart sinks. He proclaims, "Then on this day the north stands alone."

"A *Brond* never stands alone, Erlann," Strongbridge says with quiet determination as Erlann listens.

"From the gates of burning south to the mountains of the white north; call them, and they will answer."

Erlann understands what he must do.

One of Strongbridge's guards opens the door to the hall as Lady Strongbridge places her hand over her heart. "*Staerd Stern*, Erlann."

"*Staerd Stern*," Erlann responds.

The Stune Folc lock him out on the inside of the keep. Erlann prepares for a fight as he hears the sound of footsteps thumping down the hall. But it's not Thane's men who emerge. The *Brond Voldur* round the corner carrying a locked chest in their arms. The *First Spear* marches in front with a look of stubborn determination on his face.

Erlann calls to him, "*First Spear*, what news?"

"Join us up top, boy; *Baldr* may not see us today, but we'll make such a ruckus he'll hear us just the same."

Erlann clenches his fists and follows the men down the hall.

The courtyard, once a vicious battleground, has transformed into a gruesome place of execution. The victorious *Stafntaki* move with ruthless efficiency as the wounded guards writhe upon the ground. Thane's men deliver death to those on the brink, striking final blows with callous bloodlust; a ghoulish sight of wanton carnage. Thane moves through the macabre scene with quiet approval. Striding forward, the weight of his presence charges the air with inevitability as he approaches the imposing doors of *Stalden Keep*.

Inside the keep, the remaining guards can only listen helplessly from behind the high walls and locked doors. The agonizing cries mix with the cruel laughter of Thane's men, creating a symphony of horror assaulting the air.

Then, Thane kicks the doors of the keep . . . hard.

The shockwave ripples through the reinforced door. Though it bends, it does not break, thanks to the masterful craftsmanship of the *Brondsmiths* of *Alstead long ago.*

Thane turns and yells, "Ram!"

Geir hurls his throwing axe into the face of a wounded guard, then scolds the surrounding *Stafntaki*. "The ram should be up here already. Bring it forth!"

Erlann, with the *First Spear* and *Brond Voldur*, carry a chest to the center of the roof. They quickly crack it open, revealing a cache of arrows and swords. The *First Spear* laughs, and says, "'Bout time. Was never the religious sort anyway."

The *First Spear* tosses a bow to Erlann as his men take positions. Erlann aims down the bow shaft, observing a giant ram being rolled toward the main doors of *Stalden Keep*. It's a perfect shot. Erlann draws back. Suddenly, he sees Rolf writhing and contorting. He's tied to the front of the ram, being used as a human shield.

"Rolf!" shouts Erlann as he runs for the stairs, bow in hand.

The *First Spear* sees it too. "*Baldr*'s Wounds! Hold men! Hold!"

The archers relax their bows as the *First Spear* sees more wagons coming up the pass. They have hostages of their own tied across them.

Nothing more can be done from the roof. Erlann hustles down the halls of the keep. He hears the scraping sound of wood being dragged and rearranged. The guards, fueled by a mixture of adrenaline and determination, desperately attempt to hold the main doors against Thane's men who hammer against them from the outside. Working with urgency, they stack the heavy tables of the hall, constructing a makeshift barricade to forestall the coming battering ram. The first hall, once a place of solace, is now transforming into an improvised fortress as the defenders brace themselves for the coming assault.

The atmosphere within the keep is tense, punctuated by the distant sounds of Thane's forces preparing to strike. As the makeshift barricade is completed, the defenders exchange quick glances, silently acknowledging the gravity of their situation.

BANG!

The first hit of the ram comes. Erlann stands watching, not knowing what to do.

"Erlann!" shouts Tyr.

BANG!

Erlann turns and sees Tyr approaching the company with Halmar beside him. Nils and Marin follow closely behind as the *Brond Helms* survey the situation. Though the room seems secure for now, they know their disadvantage is grave.

"Our swords!" laments Halmar.

Nils answers, "They're still locked in the hall!"

Tyr grabs Erlann, and asks, "Where is your brother?"

Erlann shakes his head. He doesn't have the heart to tell his father Rolf's been taken.

BANG!

Tyr understands without words, and commands, "Go to my chambers."

"But Father," Erlann deflates.

Tyr yelps, "Now!"

Erlann stands his ground.

"Sword or no! I will bleed with you."

BANG!

Tyr puts his hand on Erlann's shoulder and nods knowingly. He has a mission for him after all, and perhaps the most important.

"Go to the main hall. At the eclipse's end, when the lock opens, bring us our swords."

Erlann nods intensely and takes off running down the hall. Tyr smiles after him for a brief moment and then turns to his fellow warriors.

Tyr roars, "*Brond* to me!"

Halmar's voice fills with concern, "We've no weapons at all!"

Tyr's face fills with a wily smile, and he responds, "Weapons? A *Brond* is a weapon."

With a single pull, Tyr breaks off a leg from one of the tables and swings it across his body. *Brond Helm* Nils smirks as he realizes the potential of this makeshift club. The other warriors begin making improvised weapons from anything and everything they can find in the first hall.

Erlann pushes open the double doors to the mead hall, yet, he's stopped cold in his tracks by an appalling sight. He sees The Caller from before; the old man is dead on the floor—his throat has been cut. The *Horn of*

Hearth rests in his hands, his charge safeguarded until the last. He died a *Brond Here*, but still, Erlann is heavily affected by the murder of this harmless old man who is long past his fighting days.

Erlann looks beyond this atrocity and notices Herald Egil standing by the stone locks, admiring the impounded swords.

"The sword of Tyr, Boon of *Stor Doren*. Tell me true, was it made in the fires of the mountain?"

Egil reaches for the sword. Erlann SCREAMS as he draws back his bow, launching an arrow at him with great speed! Egil dodges and pulls his robe back, revealing his sword. He parries Erlann's second attack as another arrow flies through the air.

Herald Egil snarls, "You should have accepted my gift."

Just then, Erlann spies a sturdy metal poker leaning against the stone of the great fireplace. *If I cannot go around*, thinks Erlann, *then I will charge through!* He quickly snatches the poker and closes the distance with Egil, ROARING as he attacks with an overhead swing.

Erlann rages as he strikes again and again, one blow after another landing and sparking on the metal of Egil's sword.

"You will NEVER break the stone, and you will NEVER defeat that lock!"

"Ah, but I have the key!" Egil retorts with a smile.

Egil counters Erlann's blow, deflecting the poker harmlessly to the side. In one swift move, Egil pulls Erlann inward, locking him into a chokehold.

"I've been waiting for you, Erlann. It's been said only the blood of the Once Queen can open this lock before the end of the eclipse." Egil smiles, and says, "Let us hope you have enough blood in common."

Egil runs his sword down Erlann's forearm, razoring a long, shallow cut. Blood droplets patter onto the ground, pooling and flowing downward into the lock and cracks on the floor.

Erlann's heart sinks as the mechanism springs to life, its gears turning and opening.

"Look and despair," hisses Egil, "for this day, *Stalden Keep* goes to King Thane!"

The swords fall out of their locking stones one by one. Erlann stomps on Egil's foot, who winces, losing his sword. Egil shoves Erlann to the floor in frustration.

"Enough foolishness!" Egil scolds.

From the ground, Erlann notices that Axel has entered the room. Axel takes up Tyr's sword from the floor, checking its balance. It's surprisingly light for a battle sword.

Erlann points his finger at Egil, yelling, "*Brond Helm!* Thane's herald is stealing the swords!"

Axel speaks calmly while brandishing Tyr's sword, "I have always cared for your family, Erlann. But today, my son walks as a free man, his ransom paid—"

"With the blood of *Alstead*," Egil finishes grimly.

Erlann gasps as Axel tosses Tyr's sword to Egil. While Axel tries to collect the swords scattered about the floor, Egil slowly closes in on an unarmed Erlann ready to finish his dark day's work.

Erlann can't believe it. This is treason of the blackest sort.

"TRAITORS! BETRAYER'S ALL!"

If Erlann could spit fire, he'd have burnt them both to ash here and now. Erlann spies Egil's sword from their previous fight, laying on the ground behind him as he approaches.

Egil answers, "Spend time in the Howling pits, and then talk to us of loyalty! Soon your brother will learn of this." Egil slashes widely at Erlann, who dodges with a forward roll across the floor, grabbing the sword behind Egil.

Erlann rises with the point toward Egil, and demands, "What of my brother? Speak!"

The sound of swords clangs and clatters in the hall as Erlann and Egil battle for their lives. Frustrated, Egil lunges and stabs at Erlann. But Erlann punches Egil with his free hand as the man sails past, causing Egil's cowl to fall back, unmasking him. Egil's face, once handsome, is now a nightmarish, crisscrossed patchwork of scars and burns, evidence of the endless torture his masters used to break him away from the loyalties of his previous life; his original family and hearth—usurped by pain. Egil squeals in shame as he strikes back, but Erlann is ready, and as they lock blades, he gets the better of his sword's position. All he need do is slide down Egil's deadlocked blade and into his black heart.

Egil pleads, "Please, young *Brond* . . . don't."

Erlann looks closer at the sword in his hand—Egil's blade; it shines with a viscous liquid almost undetectable to the eye.

"What's on this blade? What have you done to Rolf?"

Egil explains, "Poison. Though I doubt we could have added much more venom between you two brothers if we had tried."

Erlann pushes the sharp tip of his sword closer to Egil's chest. He will know not to test him.

Egil warns, breathlessly, "It incapacitates the body, but the eyes still see all. Rolf will be a mute witness to the death of your house."

Axel approaches aggressively with a stack of swords in his arms. "Enough! We must finish this!"

"Indeed!" Erlann abruptly pulls Egil out of the way, slashing toward Axel's face with the poisoned sword!

Axel quickly dodges the sword, discovering a superficial cut on his hand. He shoots his co-conspirator a look as something glows under Egil's cloak.

Axel speaks hatefully, "Son. Kill. Him."

"Brother?" Loa's soft voice cuts through the tension, immediately catching the notice of everyone in the room.

She stands in the doorway, holding the other half of the bracelet as it illuminates the dark. Axel, caught by complete surprise, is struck dumb by this development as he drops the swords in his arms. Erlann and Egil push off of each other when they see her, backing away to achieve a distance.

No one speaks as the battle lines redraw themselves.

Loa looks upon her brother's traumatized face. His appearance reflects a lifetime of torture in only a few short spans. Egil recoils from her, trying to hide his monstrous face in shame. In that moment, Loa realizes what her family has done, and that her father and brother's actions are more grotesque than any face could ever be.

Loa keeps eye contact with her father and brother as she slowly backs up. Of all the folk of Northland, she feels that she has been the most cheated.

Knowing this, Egil reaches out to her, calling, "Sister!"

Heartbroken, Loa waves him off. She studies them all, but words cannot repair what has been broken this day. Yet, when her eyes meet Erlann's, the disappointment is too much. She looks away and rushes from the room with great haste.

Axel yells, "Daughter! Stop!"

Their plan has failed. Axel charges after her as Egil collapses onto the floor with despair. Erlann steals a look at The *Horn of Hearth*; cradled in the dead Caller's hands, it's close by, almost reachable. Egil raises his head; there is murder in his eyes.

"You . . ."

He crawls back onto his feet and rises toward Erlann. Lifting Tyr's sword high above his head, Egil stretches back for a strong killing blow; his voice, the harbinger of this violent intention, "This is because of you!"

Erlann quickly grabs the horn from the floor. He finds the mouthpiece and BLOWS . . . the keep shakes as it would in a violent earthquake. Egil, standing right in front of the horn, is caught by its powerful shockwave. His screams of pain are utterly drowned out by this torrent of sound. Egil holds his ears in futility as the noise pushes him backward. His shattered eardrums run with blood; gore pours from every orifice of his body as his insides liquefy. Dead on his feet, he falls backward. His body breaks through the window behind him as he falls into the open air.

Erlann loses sight of Egil's body as he runs to the shattered window. From this great height, the wind catches his hair immediately as he scans the city below. Even in all this fighting, a confused crowd rushes to the man's aid. But there's nothing to be done. Erlann sees that Egil is dead, his body lays still on the road, with the second half of Loa's amulet in his hand.

CHAPTER 17

OF BLOOD AND BROND

T yr, Nils, Halmar, and their company strain to hold the main doors of *Stalden Keep* against Thane's forces. The battering ram mercilessly pounds the reinforced door, its tip splintering the wood with each brutal strike. Undeterred, Tyr releases a defiant growl, his muscles straining as he holds the door against the invading horde.

Amid the chaos, Erlann sprints toward the highest parapet of *Stalden Keep*. From this vantage point, he tracks the unfolding siege below. The wagons are fully unloaded, with hundreds of *Stafntaki* buzzing into the courtyard as they try to claw their way inside. In spite of all this violence, the hostages still live. Rolf still lives, at least for now.

The *First Spear* barks orders to his men from up high, keeping a steady stream of arrows raining down from his host. Even with fewer warriors, they'll need to fight nonetheless when the keep's doors are breached. With a deep breath, Erlann raises his voice above the clamor.

"For the Caller of the Keep!"

His proclamation echoes through the yard, its a rallying cry that pierces through the chaos and uncertainty. As the besieged defenders draw strength from Erlann's words, he takes a deep breath and blows the horn, signaling a call for help that resonates to the farthest reaches of Northland.

All across the land, the free folk of the North heed the call of Erlann's horn. A blacksmith turns toward the distant citadel, dropping his hammer and grabbing his sword. Farmers drop their pitchforks and pull swords out from the hay. A ship's crew turns about on the river, bearing toward *Alstead*. The call resounds even through the Great In-Between—as Elda floats through the darkness, listening to the familiar sound.

A hand rests on Erlann's shoulder as the *First Spear* smiles at him. He and the other men of the *Brond Voldur* are repositioning for a better angle on the enemy below.

"Well done, boy. Thank *Baldr* for you!"

Inside the keep, one of Thane's warriors tries to stab Tyr through a newly bashed hole in the door. Tyr claps his hands together, stopping the sword mid-stab. He then pushes it back, smashing his attacker in the face with the butt of his own pommel.

As the chaos ensues, Nils and Halmar swiftly respond to the situation. Nils, with his powerful frame, braces the barricade, reinforcing it against the relentless pounding of Thane's battering ram. Halmar darts around the area, spying the *Stafntaki* outside and marking their movements. For his comrades, he becomes a vital well of information. For the usurpers, he's a nemesis screaming abuse and insult.

Erlann strides toward them from down the hall. He wears a satchel with the *Horn of Hearth* around one shoulder. On the other shoulder, he carries a thick sack that clangs and bounces as he rushes toward the warriors.

"Father!"

Erlann drops the large sack in front of the *Brond Helm* and company. It's their swords from the hall and the storage room, as many as Erlann could carry.

"Father, I may not be allowed to hold a sword, but no rule forbids me from moving them," Erlann says, admiring the bag with quiet defiance.

Tyr's heart soars at this most welcome sight. "Good lad!"

The *Brond* gather their swords from the ground, reclaiming their hopes as well. Now they can use their mastery in full. If they cannot have victory this day, then perhaps a bard will find their deaths worthy of a song.

Erlann looks over at Marin, who's receiving last-minute advice from her father, Nils.

"If they do this, you do that."

He shows Marin a new counter-move as she listens with a look of pride on her face. Whatever happens, this is her father, a *Brond Helm* of the Free North.

The *Brond* back away from the failing doors of the keep as Tyr steps to the front of the vanguard. He raises his sword to gather their attention.

"For the liberty to speak!"

"For the freedom to keep your own!"

"For laws that stand above men, and for justice that bends not to power."

Erlann brings his horn to the ready position as Tyr nods for him to proceed. There's a look in Tyr's eye that catches Erlann's attention. It's a dignity and self-respect that only a free man can possess. In this instant, he knows that he has made his father proud.

Erlann takes a deep breath and blows into the *Horn of Hearth*. Stones rattle and shake as its sound rises in the keep.

On the other side of the doors, Thane's men hold their ears in pain—heads pound as eardrums burst. The gates of the keep blast off their hinges, crushing and sweeping away Thane's best warriors.

Recovering from this unexpected hurricane, Thane surveys the black plume of dust. The attack pauses as his men reform their battle ranks a short distance away, waiting for the air to clear. As it does, Tyr stands in the threshold, his sword at the ready.

"Free folk of Northland! Speak your mind!"

Tyr points his sword and the *Brond* roar into action.

The *Brond* explode through the threshold of *Stalden Keep* and rush down its steps into the courtyard. Thane's warriors, stunned by the previous shockwave, are caught unprepared in this charge. The front ranks are cut down either by the *Brond Voldur* or the *Brond Helm*, who follow in their wake.

Chopping down another opponent, Tyr turns. He waves his arms to get Erlann's attention through a soundscape of brutality.

"Erlann! Stafntaki press our side!!"

Erlann looks just in time to see Thane's men charging down on their flank. He quickly places the horn to his lips, and he blows out loudly! The charging men fly back, leaving none standing. This clears a new path, through which Erlann sees his brother.

Rolf's still tied to what's left of the ram, and though worse for wear, he's still very much alive. Unconscious, he pulls against his ropes as if trying to wake from an unwelcome night terror. The way is largely unopposed, so Erlann hazards an approach. He swiftly sprints across the battlefield dispatching several enemies as he works his way to Rolf's side.

Reaching him, Erlann tugs at Rolf's ropes, attempting to untie them, but they hold fast and will not yield his brother. He rocks the carriage up and down with increasing strength as he urgently tries to solve the knot.

Then, Rolf comes to and faintly says, "Erlann?"

He looks down at his bonds.

Rolf responds with his usual condescending tone, "Brother. What are you doing?"

Erlann speaks with frustration, "Hold still. I cannot loosen the knot."

Rolf looks around. He sees a fight going on. With his head, he motions to the hidden dagger on his belt.

"Cut it! My dagger, fool!"

Relief washes over Erlann's face as he draws the dagger.

Erlann speaks, "Our first battle, Rolf, and you're sleeping through it!"

Rolf's eyes widen. Erlann's right! He has to get loose!

Erlann cuts his bonds as a very groggy Rolf attacks the first enemy he can get his hands on. It's a move more reminiscent of a tavern brawl than a battlefield as they roll around in the mud.

Tyr's battle-hardened gaze sweeps across the chaos of the courtyard, his movements are fluid and purposeful as he dispatches another berserker with stoic precision. Amidst the melee, Tyr spots his two sons, Erlann and Rolf, fighting side by side with unexpected solidarity. A surge of pride wells within him as he calls to his boys across the fighting ground.

"MY SONS!"

With a pointed gesture, he singles out this remarkable display of courage in the heart of the melee. The *Brond Voldur* cheer in response to Tyr's words, a testament to the fierce determination of these stalwart defenders. But this aggressive move has not gone unnoticed, and Geir has an increasing body count of his own. He locks in on the two brothers and slowly pulls another throwing axe from his sleeve. It's the perfect opportunity to add two more scalps to his belt.

Geir prepares to strike, setting his balance when Erlann sees him. Unaware of Geir's earlier betrayal, Erlann lowers his horn with a friendly nod as he turns to other matters. Rolf notices Geir's proximity to Erlann as he turns from his latest kill.

"Erlann!" Rolf gasps.

Rolf's path is blocked by Thane's berserkers, who try to overpower him. He skillfully parries their attacks and presses forward with urgency. Taking the offensive, he slashes his way through the *Stafntaki*, determined to reach his brother. With a swift and forceful swing, he knocks his last opponent aside.

Geir smugly reaches back for a killing throw. He wears a malicious smile, as sharp as his axe.

"Child's play," he mutters while releasing his weapon into the air, turning end over end in Erlann's direction.

With no time to react, Erlann realizes too late that he's on the chopping block. Unexpectedly, Rolf tackles Erlann out of the way just in time as Geir's axe sails past them overhead.

Rolf kneels over Erlann, seeing the confused look in his eyes.

"Meet our good cousin, Geir."

Geir gives Erlann a sardonic grin, smiling awkwardly as he dips into an exaggerated bow.

"Greetings!"

He jerks his arms upward in a flash, leading Erlann and Rolf to flinch for another attack, but they quickly realize Geir's hands are empty as he waves at them. Geir tightens his fist and points to Thane who Rolf realizes is directly behind him! Before anyone has a chance to react, Thane grabs Rolf by the back of his shirt and holds him up high in the air.

Thane's voice resonates throughout the courtyard, cutting through the maelstrom.

"TYR!!!"

The chaos on the battlefield grinds to a halt as the clash of swords and the scream of war cries dissipates. As suddenly as it began, all the fighting dissolves into a palpable silence. Amid the swirling dust and glorious dead, steps Tyr. Emerging from the crowd, his imposing figure is spattered with the blood of *Stafntaki* as his boots crunch through the mud of the courtyard. The surviving *Brond Voldur* cast wary glances as their formidable champion makes his way to the front.

Thane speaks quietly now, but with no less intensity, "Where is the Queen?"

Tyr responds, "The Once Queen is not here, brother. Nor is what you seek ours to give."

The *Brond Voldur* grunt in agreement.

Thane smiles, and adds with a lilt in his voice, "Then the old saying is true: something given, nothing gained!"

It's a passphrase. On Thane's cue, Axel's men begin killing Tyr's guards on the parapet. Caught by complete surprise, some are run through from behind. Others put up a hopeless fight as they are surrounded, caught completely unaware by this second ambush.

"Axel." Tyr's heart sinks.

"Treachery!" shouts Halmar.

The *First Spear* resists the attacks of Axel's men on the roof, but there's nothing he can do for Tyr's fighters caught in the ambush. He shepherds those who remain with great skill and experience as they escape toward the roof access. He and a handful of guards fall back into one of the tower gates, barring entry to Axel's men. Erlann gazes upward as the cheers of his comrades fill the courtyard; the *First Spear* has saved *Stalden Keep* for the moment, trapping the turncoats on the roof.

Below, in the courtyard, *Brond Helm* Nils has been fighting back-to-back with his daughter, Marin. He boasts a challenge to Axel's men on the high wall.

"Cowards! Jump down here where we can kill you!"

The *Brond* let out a hearty, fearless laugh, as Northlander's do.

Thane stares at Tyr, and asks, "You know what I seek. Where's the crown?"

Axel's men rush back to the battlement and aim their bows over the stone toward Erlann and company. It's a terrible disadvantage for Tyr's warriors below, and perhaps certain death. Trying not to draw attention, Erlann slowly raises his horn to fight back. He brings the mouthpiece to his lips. Tyr, though, sees Erlann's intent and stops him by placing his hand on the horn, lowering the arcane device before Erlann can strike. Tyr glares at Thane and makes his move toward the would-be king.

"There's only one coward here. The one who hides behind a boy."

Thane's eyes narrow, and his challenging voice proclaims, "Come for him, then."

Thane pushes Rolf over to Tyr.

"Son." Tyr studies Rolf's condition.

Rolf nods that he's alright as Tyr turns to Erlann.

"See to your brother."

Erlann responds with duty in his heart, "Yes, Father. May the spirit of *Baldr* guide you on the path."

Thane sneers, "Yes, pray to your dead god. *Baldr* will not hear you, and with *Iz* eclipsed, he cannot save you."

Thane dumps his armor on the ground. His skin boasts a muscular build, strewn with the scars of many battles.

"But my god is Fenreir."

Geir smiles in admiration.

"Devourer of worlds. He makes us strong and swift."

Tyr smirks. "You don't scare me, pup. Come on then!"

The onlookers are transfixed with the unfolding spectacle as two of the greatest warriors of Northland prepare to duel. An unbearable tension builds in the air as Erlann and Rolf helplessly watch from the sidelines. Thane breaks the quiet first and with a violent growl, lunges at Tyr. His attacks are primal, fueled by raw strength and aggression, he fights with the ferocity of a wild animal unchained. Yet Tyr responds with a dance of skill and finesse, effortlessly evading Thane's brutal strikes and countering with attacks of his own. With each calculated movement, Tyr maintains his composure and confidence, unwavering even in the face of Thane's animosity.

"Finish him, Father!" yells Rolf.

Nils smiles. "Send Thane back to *The Morass*!"

Thane goes for a top blow, but Tyr swiftly swipes at Thane's midsection, cutting him. Rolf taps Erlann's shoulder and makes a gesture to watch Geir, but Erlann sees that Geir is too focused on this duel to be a threat at present. Thane and Tyr lock weapons as they push against each other.

"Give me the crown!" Thane hisses.

He leaps back just in time to escape Tyr's counter-strike, as Tyr vaults forward with a top slice blocked in turn by Thane's hammer.

BOOM!

Tyr's sword connects with Thane's war hammer, shattering it into a thousand pieces. Losing his balance, the man who would be king falls onto his back with an expression of utter shock and disbelief. As he lays in the pieces of his broken weapon, a gash opens upon his face. Erlann sighs in relief from a few feet away. Tyr lowers his weapon as Thane looks down at his, revealing the remains of a broken hilt.

"No! This isn't over!"

Thane drinks from the vial around his neck.

"More."

"MORE!"

Thane gulps down the entire vial, then, finding it empty, he rips it from his neck. Crushing the vial in his hand, he doubles over in excruciating pain. His muscles ripple and throb, his eyes turn black as he rises; the ground itself seems to quake in fear as he plants his feet upon it.

"Thane." Tyr backs away in quiet horror. "What have you done?"

"Father? " Rolf whispers with trepidation.

Tyr sees the panic on his sons' faces as he motions for them to stay back.

Then, Erlann sees Thane lunge toward Tyr with incredible speed.

Erlann tries to warn him, yelling, "Father!"

Thane strikes with a transformed, claw-like hand. His strong fingers and razor-sharp nails lash out with such force and speed that it takes off Tyr's arm with one swipe. Tyr looks down at the mangled stub which used to be his arm just a moment ago with complete shock. His labored breathing rasps in and out as sporadic gasps escape from the assembled warriors.

A low, guttural growl radiates from Thane's throat, GRRRRRRRRRR-RRRRRRRRR!!!

Erlann and Rolf scream as he kicks Tyr, who flies back and hits the wall of the keep with a force so strong it splinters the stones. Tyr lands on the steps, barely conscious as he looks toward his sons who run to his side.

Tyr struggles to speak. "My sons, look for me . . . in the Halls of *Iz*." Tyr coughs up blood with a proud smile.

"But Father, you cannot pass now!" Erlann speaks through tears.

"The eclipse still waxes!" Rolf says.

Tyr reaches for them, saying, "Fear not, boys. *Baldr* has seen me often and knows me well." Tyr smiles proudly. "Fight well, boys, and follow."

All is still as the veterans of both sides look on, a moment of frailty in the cold wind of Northland.

"Today!" Geir breaks the silence. "This war ends! DEATH TO THE HOUSE OF STALDEN!" The front ranks of Thane's *Stafntaki* reenergize and charge.

Rolf ROARS at the incoming *Stafntaki*, brandishing his sword, as if his scream alone would cleave through them. Lo, then, does the *Horn of Hearth* sound in the courtyard once again. The pure rage Erlann feels surely matches his brother's as he blows away the front ranks of the *Stafntaki*, revealing Thane behind them.

Erlann's stunned. Thane took the blast like it was nothing. Erlann watches Thane approach with alarm. He'll try again. This time, Erlann focuses solely on Thane, blowing the horn with all his might, but the shockwave has little effect on his uncle.

Thane leads the remaining *Stafntaki* up the stairs as Erlann grabs Rolf, trying to guide him inside.

Rolf brushes Erlann's arm from his shoulder, and screams, "A *Brond Here* does not run!"

Erlann shoves Rolf toward the doorway of the keep, saying, "Then it's good I'm not a *Brond Here*!"

The boys run back into *Stalden Keep* while Thane's berserkers close in from behind. As the brothers cross the threshold, Rolf looks up, calling attention to the ceiling. Erlann understands, raising his horn and pointing it toward the ceiling stones. The call of the horn blasts into the overhead stones, causing the entrance to collapse. Tyr's chamber rumbles upstairs as the commissioned mosaic sinks downward on its easel, imploding into the rubble.

As a plume of stone powder and dust clears, Erlann looks through to the completed portrait that has surfaced from the broken heap of stones that have caved-in, blocking the entrance of the keep. He sees a depiction of Tyr on the crushed canvas, his arms around his two sons with a look of pride on his face. Confronted with this ideal family portrait, Erlann's hit with a weight that could have been all the bricks of *Stalden Keep* itself.

On the outside of the keep, Thane rushes into the pile of rubble. He digs relentlessly, moving aside large boulders as if they were child's toys. Geir looks at this new unexpected obstacle with an annoyed expression on his face. As he retrieves a few of his throwing axes from the fallen dead, he realizes that even at this speed, it will take his father time to clear a path.

Tyr rests with his back on the steps. Though heavily wounded, he's amused by the site of his two sons getting the best of an entire army.

"Nephew." He addresses Geir with a weak smile. "May my sons give you as much trouble as they gave me."

Geir scowls at Tyr, who smiles back with a chuckle as the life drains from his eyes.

Then, Geir turns to a group of *Stafntaki* who await his orders.

"Follow," Geir says darkly. "There's more than one way into *Stalden*."

CHAPTER 18

KING OF ASHES

Erlann and Rolf rush through the catacombs that twist through the depths of *Stalden Keep*.

Erlann shouts, "Get the crown!"

"Yes," Rolf agrees. "Let's cast it into the river."

"Or bash it flat with a rock," Erlann adds.

They hear the sound of quiet snarling as a blade whips out from the darkness, swinging straight for Erlann's head.

"Drop!" Rolf instructs.

Erlann ducks as Rolf parries this blade. Two *Stafntaki* leap out of the darkness as Rolf swings his sword with a nimble aggressiveness. Seizing the momentum, Rolf pushes them backward. Wanting to assist, Erlann puts the *Horn of Hearth* to his lips.

CRASH! A throwing axe strikes the horn, piercing it in several places. "Silence!" Geir rasps. He jumps out from the shadows and kicks Erlann who tumbles to the floor.

Geir calls to the other *Stafntaki*, "You see, boys! Pull up enough rocks, and you can always find where the worms are hiding!"

Rolf sees what's happening, but he has problems of his own as the two *Stafntaki* block his path to Erlann.

"Daddy wants the crown," Geir says mockingly as he swings his fists ruthlessly.

Erlann covers his head as he tries in vain to protect himself on the hard floor.

"Fine!" Geir pummels Erlann with kicks and punches. "He can have it!"

Rolf fights with fierce determination, trying to close the distance between his brother and himself. Erlann notices that Geir's throwing axe is embedded in the horn. He tries to reach it, but Geir stomps down, pinning the blade to the ground.

"Bloodlines, successions, I don't see what all the fuss is about, really," Geir says as he sneers and circles to Erlann's other side. "Crown or no crown, when you kick a man, he stays down." He stomps Erlann to the floor. "Pressure him enough. Beat him enough, and he does what you say, every time."

Groggy from multiple blows, Erlann struggles to find his footing.

Geir mocks him with a sneering command, "Now, cousin, heel!"

He delivers a sharp kick to Erlann's face, sending him sprawling backward onto the floor. Despite this, Erlann manages to rise again, defiant.

"Heel!" Geir kicks him to the floor again. "Of course, some dogs can't be trained." Geir pulls another throwing axe. He has an idea. "I know! Play dead!"

Geir swings his axe downward as Erlann braces for its sharp impact.

CLANG! Geir looks up into Rolf's face, who has parried the attack. Geir glances back to find his two Stafntaki berserkers laying defeated on the hard floor.

Rolf's very proud of himself and can't resist a quick taunt, "Down, boys."

"Wolf! Wolf!" Geir barks. "Hahahaha!"

Rolf shoves Geir away from Erlann, who immediately counters by tossing another axe at Rolf. Rolf easily deflects Geir's axe with his sword as Erlann rises.

Rolf shouts to Erlann, "Go brother. Get to the crown!"

Erlann doesn't want to leave Rolf in the middle of this fight.

"Go, brother!" Rolf insists as he pulls his dagger with his off-hand and smiles sarcastically, "Geir and I must engage in noble fellowship to strengthen our family bonds."

No time to delay, Erlann turns and runs down the passage.

Up top, Thane bursts through the debris blocking the entrance of the keep. He leads a fierce band of warriors as they charge down the dimly lit hall. With each step, Thane's imposing figure grows larger as his silhouette casts a long shadow against the flickering torchlight. His eyes gleam with a ruthless determination. He has never been so close to his prize.

Erlann stands in front of the ancient throne room, frozen in place, listening. The two guards who previously stood watch over this room have been butchered by an unknown party inside.

"Daughter, come out!" He hears Axel's voice.

Loa responds, "The House of Stalden has ever been our friend."

Axel snaps back. "Loa!"

Erlann slips into the throne room as quietly as possible. He sees Axel at the other end, now drunk and disoriented from the poison's effects. He's searching for Loa—covered in the blood of the guards he just killed. The echo in the chamber makes it difficult for him to fix her location.

"You lied to me, Father!" Loa's voice levels a dagger of contempt.

"To protect you! So we could be a family again!" Axel finds her hiding behind one of the columns and quickly grabs her arm.

"Let go!" Loa yells while pulling free from his grip. "How many other families did you destroy today?" She backs toward the throne, unmindful of the trap. "Too many, it seems, and all for your son?" Loa digs in, "Seems a poor bargain."

She steps into the edge of the light beam shrouding the crown and throne.

Erlann leans in, knowing he must warn her.

BOOM!!!!!

Thane kicks in both doors as he enters the royal hall. Then, he stops unexpectedly, as if taking in the moment. After so many spans, so much struggle, his homecoming is complete. He spies the crown in the center of the room, glistening on the throne.

"The seat of the Queen, at last."

Axel stammers, "K-King Thane."

Noting the distraction, Erlann quietly steps out of the shadows from behind Loa. He takes great care not to startle her.

"Loa. Tell me true—"

She turns and looks deeply into Erlann's eyes, speaking with utter sincerity, "I knew nothing of this, Erlann, I swear on *Baldr's* name."

Erlann takes her hand, and gently says, "Come. We must be swift."

Thane approaches Axel, who's almost delirious from the poison.

"The swords! We lost the swords."

Thane speaks quietly, "It matters not. *Alstead* is mine now and soon all of Northland will bow low."

"What of my son?" Axel questions. "Will you release him to me?"

"Axel," Thane purrs, "May I share a secret with you? There were never any hostages to release. All who are taken sooner or later recognize their error and take up the sword for the true king of Northland. You've been battling many of them this day."

Axel recoils.

Thane softens his tone, saying, "Fear not. Your family will be remembered for a thousand spans in this story of my victory. Now, hold fast to me as your king."

Axel hesitates for a second but cannot refuse his king. He steps forward into Thane's embrace. Thane pulls Axel closer, his grip getting tighter every second as Axel's armor collapses inward.

Erlann approaches the throne with cautious and deliberate movements. He extends his hand carefully, mindful of the intricate network of light beams guarding Elda's crown. With a steady hand, he maneuvers slowly, skillfully navigating the shifting patterns of light. He avoids triggering the trap, but the crown remains out-of-reach of his frustrated fingers.

Loa hears the screeching sound of bending metal. She looks toward her father and sees that Axel is being crushed in Thane's merciless grasp. With a sickening thud, Thane drops Axel's lifeless body on the hard, ungiving floor.

"Father!" Loa's anguished cry fills the chamber. Hearing this, Thane's attention shifts toward Erlann, who pulls the crown into his arms, defeating the trap. Erlann returns Thane's gaze with a fiery resolve.

Erlann's voice is urgent yet composed, "Loa, we have to go."

He sees that Thane is blocking the only way out. Loa stands frozen, but she's not afraid; instead, she stands in mournful shock of a world too cruel to bear. Erlann watches Thane move toward them, their escape route blocked. Thane's imposing figure looms between them and the only path to safety.

Back in the courtyard, Marin and Nils fight alongside pockets of the remaining *Brond*. But their numbers dwindle with each fallen warrior; they are losing the fight. She sees an arrow strike Nils in the chest. It knocks the wind out of him, causing him to fall on one knee. Marin sees that Axel's men on the parapet are mercilessly picking off the *Brond* below.

"Father! Come!"

Marin helps her wounded father down the steps toward the mead cellar. But he grabs her instead.

"Go in," he says. Bar the door behind you."

Marin's repulsed by her father's words. "I'll not hide, Father!"

Nils runs his fingers through Marin's hair.

"You're as brave as any *Brond* I have ever fought with. But it's not as a *Brond Helm* that I give you this order."

Marin understands.

Nils says, "My daughter, here is my last command: fight hard, love long, and live with the sun on your face."

Marin, acknowledging his wishes, and says, "Yes, father."

Nils's expression changes to one of sternness. "In the *Halls of Iz*, there is no night."

Marin screams in protest as Nils pushes her into the cellar, slamming the door shut. She beats her fists against the door as she cries, "Father! Father!"

Marin grows quiet. She knows what she has to do but has never wanted so much to do the opposite. She turns the lock and resigns herself to the relative safety the cellar.

CHAPTER 19

FRAILTY FOR POWER

The prisoners in the throne room call to Thane, rattling their bars, screaming for release. Thane ignores them, however, focusing on his ultimate goal so close at hand. Erlann stands poised behind the throne, clutching the crown tightly in his arms, his heart pounding with anticipation. Loa lurks a few paces away, concealed behind a sturdy stone column, her eyes distant with despair as she watches the unfolding scene.

Thane sniffs the air and breathes out heavily.

"I can smell your fear, little one."

"I do not fear you," Erlann responds.

Thane smiles.

"Come now, Nephew." Thane moves closer, toward the light.

Erlann takes a step back, drawing him into the 'porcupine' trap.

"Give me the crown," Thane demands.

"Come take it, then," Erlann says as he smirks with assurance.

Stomping toward Erlann, Thane suddenly halts his advance just short of the light beam. His eyes fill with a suspicious look as he studies it.

Erlann's taken aback and he wonders, *How could he know?*

With deliberate steps, Thane navigates around the beam. Bending down, he grips a section of the stone floor, pushing his claws into the rock.

Erlann knows now that his trap has failed. He looks on helplessly as Thane's claws chip and cut through the stone like a knife through bread. Then, with incredible strength, Thane violently rips the chunk upward, flipping it down into the beam. The mechanism screeches into action, its metal blades grind against the rock, seizing the gears as the contraption breaks. Thane slyly steps safely into the light . . .

"Mother always loved her tricks."

A stone skips off the throne, pegging Thane in the face.

Erlann catches sight of Loa, her expression seething with vengeance.

"Good bounce," he quips, offering a smile in her direction.

Thane, in a fit of frustration, clutches his eye with one hand as he unleashes a furious blow upon a nearby column, smashing through it. Erlann's heart leaps into his throat as he realizes that Thane's intent is to bring the entire throne room crashing down on them.

"Run!" Erlann shouts. "Come, Loa!"

Chunks of stone rain down upon the prisoners, their anguished cries drowned out by the deafening roar of falling rocks and crumbling walls. Trapped within the side chambers, they are helpless against the cascading rubble. Desperation fills the air as they struggle against the prison bars, the cavernous chamber becoming their tomb.

Erlann and Loa must escape! As they rush past Axel's body, Loa falls to her knees, overwhelmed by the grotesque sight. She pulls Egil's bloody rune necklace from her blouse and joins it to her half of the necklace, making it whole. Erlann realizes she must have found Egil's remains on the streets below. He recognizes the runic letter at last; it's the oldest word known to their people: Othila.

"Home."

Loa speaks gently, "Go be with your family, Erlann. Tell them, Loa, daughter of Axel, was unafraid."

She looks up at Erlann, but what he sees is not reservation, but devotion. There's no time to argue. Thane's very close now. Erlann wishes he could do more.

He gives her his blessing. "May the *Halls of Iz* shine upon you, Loa."

"And on you, Erlann," Loa replies.

She looks back. Her eyes are full of longing for the life she wishes she could have had—a life with her family, a life with Erlann, a life of peace and freedom. But this was not her path.

As Erlann backs away with the crown, he takes one last look at her. Loa's expression is serene as the hall collapses around them—her face an avatar of bravery itself. Erlann breaks eye contact with a regret that crushes his heart. He uses this sorrow to fuel his stride as he sprints from the chamber.

Erlann emerges from the throne room, thinking through what he's seen. But his mind can find no words of comfort for sights so horrible. Jogging ahead, he sees a figure emerge from the dark, running toward him.

"Rolf!" Erlann speaks with relief.

"Not that way, brother!" Rolf exclaims.

Erlann peers down the hall and sees their cousin Geir charging toward them with thirty *Stafntaki* at his back. Rolf grabs Erlann's arm instead and pulls him toward the throne room.

"No! That's no good either," Erlann mutters.

In a frantic rush, Erlann drags Rolf into a nearby side crypt, his heart pounding in his chest as they slam the heavy door shut behind them. Erlann notices a peephole and peers out through the dimly lit chamber. His gaze meets that of Geir, who lurks outside the door, his smug sneer gleaming through the opening.

"Boo!" Geir laughs at Erlann's startled expression. "I thought *Brond Here* never ran from death."

Erlann is unamused, and warns, "If you seek death Geir, come in then."

"We will introduce you to him," Rolf finishes as Erlann slams the peephole closed.

Marin peeks out from the small portal set inside the cellar wall, her heart pounding with fear and anticipation. The echoes of battle have gradually diminished, replaced by the sparse clatter of swordplay and eerie moans of the wounded. With a knot of dread tightening in her stomach, she scans the piles of dead beyond, searching frantically for her father.

CRASH!

The sharp pop of a smashing bottle pierces the air, drawing Marin's attention. Laughter follows, mocking and derisive, as the remnants of a broken mead bottle spills across the floor in a small tide. Marin turns and looks deeper into the cellar. Among the many shelves she spots a man, sitting in the corner.

"Quiet, drunk!" Marin retorts sharply. "Should you not be out there?" The edge in her voice betrays her frustration.

The man raises his head and Marin is at once confronted by the gaze of *Brond Helm* Erik, a look of despair is etched deeply into his face; his eyes holding a mix of frivolity and madness.

Erik's been drinking heavily and takes yet another sip from a new mead bottle which he pulls from the shelf next to him. Marin notices Erik's complete disregard for his host's property as he sucks down another bottle, smashing its integrate glasswork against the wall with a loud pop as he finishes.

"You look for battle, girl? True death is upon us; it matters not how we die."

Marin realizes Erik is beset by the death of his son, Sven. She wonders if Erik has been here all this time?

"*Brond Helm* Erik." She speaks, "Forgive me, I didn't recognize you."

Erik pulls another mead bottle from the shelf. He pretends to read the label for a moment, but then suddenly and violently launches the full bottle at Marin, who promptly ducks away from the shattering glass.

Erik smirks, "Spare me the formalities, girl. If you're looking for a hero, you've come to the wrong cellar."

Marin listens intently as she approaches Erik, the weight of his words hang heavily on her shoulders. Erik raises his eyebrows and passes her a fresh mead bottle which she carefully accepts. Marin takes a swig from the bottle, its sweet taste brings a bitter feeling of happier days past, though for her, it offers little comfort.

Erik scoffs, "Good or evil! Liberty or slavery!"

"These are easy choices to make. But then, one day, you'll be given a new choice. Between a good . . . and that thing you love." He pauses as this impossible choice hangs heavy in the air. "Then, young *Brond Here*, you will know what it feels like to lose. Then, you will know."

Below in the catacombs, several *Stafntaki* crash against the door, trying to break it down. Erlann and Rolf hold them back with increasing difficulty as the door begins to break.

Then, Erlann hears his grandmother's voice, "Hold fast, grandson. I am coming."

Erlann turns to see Elda, reflected in a corpse's burial armor, an echo, a shadow.

He asks her, "The crown. Is it the source of all this evil?"

Elda responds, "A crown is nothing but metal and stone. A trinket—an outer symptom of an inner disease. Thane wants what all want; as if power could fill the emptiness of his heart."

"We can't stop him. We can't stop Thane," Erlann admits.

"We can! As the giant *Rasmus* began the world with a thought . . . you will end Thane's." Elda instructs, "Now listen well . . ."

Erlann inspects the wall. He notices several cracks in the stone through which water gently trickles.

On the other side of the chamber door, Thane storms forward as the *Stafntaki* fearfully clear out of his way. He kicks through the reinforced wood as if it were nothing—sending a storm of splinters into the room. This disturbs the ancient dust, creating a thick haze as Thane and company survey the room. It's empty—Erlann and Rolf are nowhere to be seen. The company holds silently, waiting for the cloud to settle. Then, through the haze, Thane notices his mother's crown resting alone on a stone coffin.

He laughs as his warriors slowly join in.

Geir places the crown on Thane's head. He's elated!

Thane shouts, "VICTORY!"

All his warriors kneel before him, hailing the king of Northland.

"Grrrrrrrrrrr-Rah!!!!!"

Erlann drops from the ceiling onto Thane's back. But something is wrong. Thane doesn't fall. Erlann bounces his weight on Thane's shoulders, trying to bring him down.

Thane swats at Erlann as one would an insect, saying, "Foolish boy!"

But as he brings his hands up, Rolf lunges from the dark.

"Hey! Tiny!"

Thane swings his fist, but Rolf ducks as Thane's punch takes apart the wall behind him. Dark water rushes into the chamber as Rolf kicks Thane's knee, buckling his weight from under him.

"For father," whispers Rolf.

Thane's knocked off balance, just enough for Erlann to push him into a fall. Erlann and Thane drop toward their reflection in a pool of water that has collected in the center of the room.

Erlann closes his eyes and speaks the sacred words, *"Se flód tíma is hweorfa."*

Time slows as the two of them crash into the water, disappearing below its surface. Geir runs up and carefully tests the puddle with the tread of his boot. It's shallow, somehow they've gone from this place.

"Father? What trickery is this?" he demands.

Rolf strides to the center of the room, sword drawn as he readies his stance. "What's wrong, Geir? Something amiss?"

Geir ROARS as his men charge into the room.

Breaking past the surface of the water, Erlann and Thane plunge headlong into the vast expanse of *The Great In-Between*. Thane grabs at Erlann, who's still on his back.

"What's this? You're like Mother with her tricks!"

Thane throws Erlann from his back, but not before Erlann grabs onto Thane's crown. He points it at Thane, mocking him as he floats away.

"You wish to be king?" He holds out the crown, baiting him.

"I am king!" Thane shouts after Erlann. "It's not your place to deny me!"

Thane sails after Erlann, who drifts into the nearest cloud. A mist swirls around them both as they enter this place of the past, present, and future. Erlann looks back and sees Thane reflected endlessly in the mirrored depths of the cloud. Different guises and possibilities, but always him.

"Give me the crown!"

Thane's sentence is thunderously echoed by all the other doppel-gängers in the vapor. He's startled by this unexpected development as he looks out upon his own reflections. For that brief moment, they all spoke in unison, but the reflections are unaware of him and continue on with their individual lives.

"What madness is this?" whispers Thane.

Erlann and Thane find themselves suddenly standing at the top of *Ensam Fjall*. The lonely mountain where all trials have ever begun. A like-ness of Elda forms out of the cloud, adorned in full battle armor—wearing her own crown. She approaches, riding on a Griffin's back. Her likeness is noticeably younger as she lands on the peak.

"Thane! What have you done this day?"

For a moment, Thane and Erlann think she's talking to them; but Erlann looks over his shoulder and sees a younger version of Thane, aged sixteen, at the cliff's edge. Erlann realizes that this is Thane's past, from his trial attempt long ago. Young Thane's face is covered in blood as he hovers over the body of his dead sister of twenty. She has been stabbed many times in the back—a vicious killing.

"She took my sword . . ." Young Thane tries to explain. "She was going to win!"

"Animal!" Elda says with scorn as she approaches on foot.

Young Thane is cut by her words. "You should be proud!" His self-righteousness wells-up from within, reaching crescendo. "I have only ever followed your example!"

Elda, for the first time in her life perhaps, is at a loss for words.

Young Thane burrows in, "Do you not crush your enemies?! Be they wicked or righteous, all must bow before the crown!"

Younger Elda stands dumbstruck; there's but one thing she can do now. She quietly approaches her young son and whispers to him, "My bold son, now, my last command I shall give to you." Her eyes narrow in equal parts grief and rage, "Remain here, and watch over your sister."

Young Thane shivers in the evening frost, his face is awash with confusion.

"Mother?"

"Shhhh. Rest now," says young Elda.

Young Thane shakes in the growing cold as the last light of the day is lost.

Elda's doppelgänger drops her war-hammer on the mountainside as she turns and walks away.

Erlann studies the dead woman on the ground, his mother, as the snowflakes fall around them. Older Thane listens intensely as the younger Elda leaves him to die in the snow. Older Thane walks next to her, keeping pace as he attempts to explain. "I did everything you asked! Lived how you wanted me to live! Killed how you wanted me to kill! You left me to die! Look now, Mother, am I not strong?"

Younger Elda doesn't respond or acknowledge Thane, as she fades into the distance as both young and old Thane call out to her in unison.

"Mother!"

Erlann realizes that Thane's mesmerized by the shadows of the cloud as it plays out his life in all its infinite possibilities. Thane's potential paths unfold before him, like scenes in a tapestry. In one shadow, Thane languishes in the confines of a dungeon—a prisoner of his own ambition. In another, he meets his end at the merciless hands of Tyr, his unforgiving executioner. In yet another shadow, he sees Thane falling on the battlefield, his life extinguished as the tide of battle rises against him. Yet, a glimmer of hope emerges in a different shadow as Thane allies with Tyr, only to see his brother-in-law ascend to the throne. Finally, Thane sees himself clutching the crown in his hands—it's the culmination of all his ambition.

Thane looks on, hopefully, and asks, "What's this?! What's this?!"

Then, all of his subjects turn away from Thane, leaving him alone with not a soul to command. Thane looks on, confused, as the countless variations of his destiny play out, yet none lead to what he desires.

Erlann whispers, "Grandmother told me. Of all your paths, and all your ends, never in any fate, uncle, will you be king."

Thane screeches, "They reject me at all turns! I'll kill them! I'll kill them all!"

The voices begin to stack in intensity, echoing Thane, almost mocking him. His path, his mindset—always led to this. Then, a familiar face forms from the vapor.

It's Tyr. He shouts, "Thane!"

Thane turns to Tyr, who's lecturing another version of Thane. Erlann notices that Thane is beginning to feel that the shadows are speaking to him.

Thane speaks with violence in his voice, "You!" He reaches for Tyr, but his hand passes through like the mist of a cloud. Tyr continues to speak, "You never bested me. You had to cheat to defeat me!"

"No!" answers Thane.

Elda forms.

"You should have died in the wilderness, murderer."

"Mother!!!!" Thane pleads.

Thane attacks the mist, but it simply dissipates and then reforms somewhere else, smothering him.

"Small," says Elda.

"Weak," seconds Tyr.

As the pressure builds, the voices repeat with relentless intensity, echoing through the tumultuous clouds. Thane's screams pierce the air as he collapses onto his knees, overwhelmed by the cacophony of unwanted accounts from his past. The swirling clouds engulf him, suffocating him with the weight of his own history, each echo a haunting reminder of his actions and choices.

Back in the catacombs, Erlann, Thane, and the crown break the water's surface. They both roll onto the floor, gasping for breath. Rolf stands over them. With unyielding determination, he has managed to hold off Geir and his followers. As Erlann and Thane emerge, a stunned silence falls over the group. The combatants pause, their attention diverted to the two men. They watch with a mixture of surprise and disbelief—their expressions betraying astonishment regardless of their allegiance.

Rolf speaks with concern in his voice. "Brother?"

"I live," answers Erlann as he rises from the water.

Geir gazes at the pitiful, crumbling figure of Thane as he cowers on the floor. The crown rests between his legs in the water, all Thane need do is reach out, and grasp it.

Geir whispers, "My king?"

Thane raises his arms, studying his unnatural claws transformed by Fenreir's blood. The cursed gore has made talons for hacking and ripping, but no hands for making or holding. He takes in the full weight of his choices, perhaps for the first time.

"Help me, my son."

Geir watches as Thane tries to lift the crown from the floor, but he can't; his nails slip and slide off the edges of the crown.

Erlann examines Thane, noticing that his uncle's spirit has been crushed by *The Great In-Between*. Thane tries desperately to pick up the crown. But, its weight is too much to bear.

Thane begs, "The crown, it slides from my hands."

In frustration, Thane pulverizes the stone floor into dust with his fist. Geir and company look on with disbelief. Stepping forward, Erlann picks up the crown. In that moment, Thane looks up and sees him as he will be: Erlann stands over Thane, dressed in black robes—a prophet of *The Great In-Between*. Confronted with this truth, Thane screams and runs for the surface, his confused son and company following closely behind. Rolf approaches Erlann with disbelief in his eyes.

Somehow, they've won.

Rolf quietly reaches out to his brother, embracing him.

He leans in and warns, "Whatever you've done today, brother, don't ever do that to me."

Erlann smiles as they give chase.

CHAPTER 20

TIDE OF LIBERTY

Through the mead cellar portal, Marin watches as many *Stafntaki* warriors retreat in haste. Creeping from within the confines of the mead cellar, she scans the courtyard determining the best moment to launch her ambush. Then she spies Thane's captain, who promptly cuts down a fleeing *Stafntaki*. His own man.

The captain stands in the middle of the courtyard, issuing his commands with a snide authority, "Put them all down. The runners. The weak. The wounded. By order of the king!"

Another *Stafntaki* drags Nils into Marin's view. She watches helplessly as her father's body slides limply across the dirt. He's been mauled badly, with multiple axe and sword cuts—a sign of the many enemies needed to bring him down. Marin swells with a warrior's pride at her father's last stand. All she can do now though is hold, watching for a sign of life from her father's slumped body. They drop Nils in the center of the dead prisoners. As Marin looks out at him through the portal, Nils feels his daughter's eyes upon him and turns to meet her gaze. Too wounded to speak, his face warns her not to go through with her plan.

Marin understands he doesn't want her to reveal herself, though this upsets her greatly. Nils turns back and looks into the face of his soon-to-be murderer—and smiles. The *Stafntaki*, unsettled by this unexpected reaction, prepares to strike.

Then they all hear it: a distant cry resounds through the air. Thane's

167

captain abruptly halts his commands, his attention drawn to the distant horizon. There, under an ancient sun, the glint of swords catches his eye—a tide of liberty surges toward the city gates, free folk racing to defend *Alstead*. They're men and women, parents and children, the very essence of North-land's strength and independence embodied in their ranks. They don't all possess swords, but it matters not to them. They charge with hammers and pitchforks, wood axes, and quarter-staffs, a formidable levy all the same.

The captain shouts to the remaining *Stafntaki*, "Close the city gate!"

In the gatehouse, Thane's men slowly turn the wheels of the massive city doors—trying to shut out these reinforcements before they arrive. Yet, as the captain's gaze lifts to the sky, an unusual sight comes into view: a large, dark silhouette, resembling a bird, looms downward in the waxing light of *Brond*, the fire moon.

It comes closer . . . closer . . .

The captain recoils in horror as a giant griffin swoops down on him. With Elda riding on its back, the griffin scoops him up in its talons and drops him onto the city. He screams to his death as he falls hundreds of feet—splattering onto the hard cobblestone below. Another two griffins land on the *Stafntaki*, who are trying to close the gate. The death cries of the men are drowned out by the pecking of beak on bone as their armor is shattered. Suddenly, there are dozens of griffins, buzzing and weaving through the city streets attacking Thane's men.

Back in *Stalden Keep*, the *Stafntaki* run for their lives in the wake of this unforeseen onslaught. Marin sees her chance and unbolts the door to the mead cellar; swinging it open. She rushes to Nils's side on the other end of the courtyard. He looks toward her, smirking proudly as the life drains from his eyes. Marin puts her hand over her chest in salute, "And it was so."

He's gone. Marin closes her father's eyes.

Then, the sound of another distant battle reaches her ears. She looks down on the city of *Alstead* and sees that the main gates are only partially open, largely frustrating the *Brond Here's* attempts to reinforce the city. Her task is clear. Marin fights her way toward the gatehouse, dispatching many enemies. Reaching the wheel that controls the gate, she gives it a strong turn. The *Brond* outside let loose a thunderous cheer as their ranks pour into the city!

The battle is over. Thane's men have been crushed by the righteous fury of the seven corners. The *Brond* round up the remaining *Stafntaki* into circles and put them under guard, awaiting further instruction.

Elda stands over Tyr's body in the courtyard, having dismounted from her griffon. Her eyes are closed in grief, as her muddy white gown blows angrily in the wind. The giant griffin she was riding stands behind her, waiting with wings folded. Elda's eyes open, they're filled with rage and retribution. Thane, helped by two *Stafntaki*, Geir, and what remains of the enemy host emerge from the rubble of the keep.

"T-H-A-N-E!!!!!" calls Elda.

Upon seeing Elda, Thane's men melt away in fear. He falls to his knees, Thane's confidence shattered by the revelation of his character.

"Mother . . . I-I," Thane's voice trails off, as words escape his grasp as well.

Erlann and Rolf emerge from the entrance, surveying the victorious scene.

Elda speaks with authority, "Since the dawning, there has been but one ruler of the Northern Lands, and there shall never be another."

Elda acknowledges Erlann as he brings her the crown.

Suddenly, Geir raises his throwing axe to strike Elda from behind. "For the king!"

Elda turns, reaching into his mind. "You have but one master now . . ."

Geir grabs his head, collapsing in searing pain.

Elda announces boldly to everyone, "Behold, Erlann. As intentions flow through men's minds, you can reflect them back; thoughts flow like a river from the Great In-Between."

Elda continues speaking . . . her words are quiet but now rip through the skulls of all Thane's men. They all keel over in extreme pain.

Erlann is torn; he looks to Rolf, who folds his arms in contempt for their enemies.

Erlann calls out to Elda, "Grandmother!"

Elda ignores him and focuses her rage on Thane and his men. "Savages.

I offered you the chance to live under Baldr's law as men, yet you chose the path of power."

Elda extends her arm as all Thane's forces fall to the ground . . . writhing and twisting, begging for death.

Erlann yells louder, "Grandmother! Please!"

Erlann raises the crown toward Elda as he makes an appeal, "I once heard a song, of a tyrant Queen, who laid down her power to end the killing. So that free folk could speak their mind and hold fast to it."

Elda releases Geir and his men from their vice of pain. They lay about in the courtyard, sprawling on the ground, recovering from the suffering that they themselves would have inflicted.

Lo, Elda takes the crown from Erlann's hands.

"I kept this in remembrance of my frailty for power, a flaw that I have ever wished to fight." Elda places the crown in the shade of the keep and speaks the shadow words, *"Se flód tíma is hweorfa . . ."*

They watch as the crown sinks into the dark of the Great In-Between.

"Our gift is a curse, Erlann."

The metal of the crown begins to corrode at an accelerated rate.

"We can see any possibility, know any future, but the past cannot be unmade."

Erlann and Elda watch from the safety of the courtyard as the crown descends into the tides of time. It ages thousands and thousands of spans in a few brief moments, disintegrating into shining dust like so many stars.

As Elda does this, the eclipse wanes. The dark red of *Brond* separates from the strong blue light of *Iz*, restoring the natural light of day as the two celestial bodies traffic away from one another in the sky. Erlann considers Elda's words: the past is set; there's no changing it. Going forward on his path, he will do all he can to make his journey worthy of stone and song.

Elda turns to Thane's faction, speaking quietly, "Fly now, sons of the wolf, before I change my mind."

Geir raises his hand, quietly commanding the *Stafntaki* to retreat. They pick up Thane and quickly head for the gates of *Alstead*, running for their lives into the wilderness of Northland beyond. The families of *Alstead* venture out from their houses and shops to find their dead with wails of sorrow; as others untie the hostages from wagons, celebrating that they are, somehow, still alive. Lady Strongbridge and her attendants are also there, having taken to the streets to help with the aftermath as best they can.

Erlann spots Marin through the crowd. She walks toward him with an exhausted smile on her face. Covered in dry dust and crimson, she's been through much—the whole city has. But they live.

"Marin?!"

Erlann reacts to the sight of her. She's a fright!

"*Freya's tears!*"

Marin bursts out laughing as they fall into each other's arms, old friends reunited, and grateful to be breathing. Erlann stops as he sees Rolf and Halmar, carrying the body of Kare out of the watch-tower by the wall. Kare's corpse is laid next to Tyr's—joining a long line of the fallen along the main road.

Erlann and Marin take in the moment; so many have been lost.

Elda speaks to the crowd, "Free folk of the north, if you will, bring your champion to me."

Erlann and Rolf jump into action, as they try to lift their father's body out of the dust.

Suddenly there are several dozen people around them.

"My arm is yours!" says one *Brond Here*.

"As is mine!" says a farmer who drops his scythe.

The *Brond* of Northland hoist Tyr upon their shoulders, and a solemn hush falls over the crowd as they line the streets. The people's heads are bowed in silent respect for their champion, offering quiet prayers and blessings; a testament of love and respect.

Tyr, the lawbringer and *Brond Helm* of *Alstead*, peacemaker of the Free North, is lifted high as the procession moves forward with dignified solemnity. As they approach Elda, Erlann turns to her with a solemn nod, his expression reflecting the gravity of the moment. The crowd secures Tyr upon the Griffin's back and then moves away in a show of respect, clearing a path for this majestic beast.

"Hold, Grandmother!"

Rolf rushes up to Elda, carrying Tyr's blade. "Father's sword!" he exclaims, and then volunteers it to Elda in a moment of great respect.

Elda thanks him with a proud smile and then motions for Erlann to approach.

"This is for you, Erlann, son of Tyr, whose perception cuts deeper than any sword. Keep it for your father with well-deserved honor, as the *Brond Helm* of *Alstead*."

Erlann's floored by the revelation of this success. He spies Lady Strongbridge in the crowd who nods her approval. It seems this battle shall be considered an *Honor Circle* by all. Erlann realizes that the final virtue of these trials; this gathering—*Honor*, is his.

Never before has a *Brond Helm's* office passed from father to son. Yet, this is not by lineage, but worth. He will oversee the application of justice in Alstead and the eastern corner beyond. Erlann's silent acceptance is taken in stride as Elda launches into the sky on the back of her griffon. Erlann watches Elda and Tyr fly off into the west on favorable winds.

Erlann notices Rolf at the edge of the crowd, his stare locked on the ill-gotten sword at his side. There's tension in Rolf's stance, a silent contemplation etched on his face. Approaching him, Erlann senses the weight of unspoken remorse hanging heavy in the air. Rolf's internal struggle is palpable amid the somber atmosphere of the crowd, their silent sorrow intensifying his own inner turmoil.

CHAPTER 21

THE CALL OF DEATH

O n the far bank of the *Grenileir*, Rolf drops his bloody sword into the water as the fire moon, *Brond,* sets in the west. He watches as the river accepts his offering, and the blade disappears beneath the waves. Then, Rolf notices Erlann, who has been watching from a distance. Erlann nods in approval, but Rolf does not acknowledge this, sulking away in shame.

Tonight, Erlann stands once again in the burning place, *bálstaðr*. He receives a torch, which he passes down to Marin. She takes a moment to look upon the face of her departed father, Nils, as well as the multitude of *Alstead* who have fallen. The attendees pass wicker torches down the line in an almost endless succession.

The fallen are dressed in full battle armor, with the exception of the younger, poorer, *Brond*. But all grasp their swords in death. Another torch reaches Erik, who refuses it as he holds his son Sven's shield in the darkness. Halmar reviews the accommodations of his dead son, Kare, laying modestly dressed in a pile straw. He stands with his head down, as if all of *Baldr's* suffering has fallen on his shoulders. Erlann notices that Kare has no sword for his journey. He looks compassionately toward Marin as he draws his own.

Halmar holds out his hand, stopping Erlann. "Brother Helm. That's not the way of the *Brond*." He pauses a moment and then draws his own magnificent sword.

"But there is also the way of fathers and sons." He places the sword in his son's arms. "For your journey."

The warriors echo their approval with a staggered benediction, "And it was so."

Halmar takes a torch from another warrior and lights Kare's pyre. They watch as the fire rises above the kindling, forming a blaze of flickering flame. With a quiet sanctity, Marin lights her father Nils's pyre as well. Erlann peers through the flames and spies, somewhat unexpectedly, the body of the caller. His old face once rosy and joyful is now pale and sunken. The man's entire body is drained and diminished of essence—only a husk remains, mocking the former warmth of his presence. The caller holds his shattered Horn of Hearth in an eternal embrace, his charge in life and death. Erlann realizes that there will never be another of its kind, this Horn of Hearth, with its maker lost to history, its keeper lost to war, *and the people of Rasmus are forever poorer for it*. Erlann looks farther past and sees many similar funeral pyres dotting the *Grenileir* river bank.

"The river burns tonight."

The funeral hearths are gently pushed into the water from the riverbank. They drift with the current, illuminating the land as they float down the river. All stand quietly on the shore, observing in respectful silence. Rolf's gaze remains fixed on the crackling embers as they dance in the water.

He growls loudly, "No fire will light Geir's journey through the Great In-Between; only choking cold, and the sound of water in his ears, as he dies in the mud of *Rasmus*. My cousin's only ode will be of the hatred for him, remembered in song."

Erlann nods his head in agreement. He begins the last words, a warrior's rite for the dead and a prayer for safe journey through the Great In-Between.

"Hail *Baldr*, Titan, Bringer of cold, from you all goodness flows."

Marin joins him.

"Bring us young and old, through breaking blow; Home to your fold."

Slam!

Erlann sees Erik banging on his son's bloody shield with his fist. The warriors of Northland join with him, slamming their shields to the rhythm of the prayer.

Slam!

Erlann joins in with his own shield.

Slam!

Rolf joins in. Then Marin. Then all. Soon, everyone is swept up in the powerful rhythm, their hearts resounding as one. Blood calls out for blood. Soon, the *Brond* of the Free North will march against their cousin Geir, and the south corner's morass will ring with the sounds of stomping boots and dying screams.

The brothers and sisters of Northland beat their swords against their shields with determined rhythm, as their loved ones are consumed by water and flame.

THE END

GRASPING AT SHADOWS

The embers dim, yet the fires of war are stoked.
What was lost in the dust of Alstead must be avenged in the frost and fury of battle, as the murmurs of the dead whisper on the winds.

For Erlann, the call of the Great In-Between grows stronger, as the boundary between life and death is hacked away. The past wears heavily upon him. He has lost much—but is it within his power to defy loss itself?

For Rolf, the scars from his lies run deep, it's a shame that time itself cannot heal. Recklessness is a poor salve for regret, yet he presses forward, determined to carve victory from his grief. Yet, how much will he sacrifice on his quest for absolution?

The horn has sounded, and the hearth still smolders. A span of spears and swords has begun.

S.P. Rowe

ISEN MUR

STOR

EINSAM FJALL

BROND

IZ

RÉN

STANHENG HOL

BÁLSTAÐR

ALSTEAD

EY SANNHET

THE WORLD OF RASMUS

The Brothers

- **Erlann:** A young warrior grappling with bravery and vulnerability, facing both supernatural and personal challenges.
- **Rolf:** Erlann's older brother, characterized by his support, adventurous spirit, and fierce loyalty.

The Brond

- **Elda:** The once-queen of Northland—Erlann and Rolf's grandmother.
- **Tyr:** The first *Brond Helm* of *Alstead* and lawgiver of Northland—father of Erlann and Rolf.
- **Nils:** A seafaring *Brond Helm* from the northeastern corner.
- **Marin:** Daughter of Nils.
- **Erik:** A *Brond Helm* from the western lands.
- **Sven:** Erik's son.
- **Halmar:** A *Brond Helm* known for his tactical skill.
- **Kare:** Son of Halmar, undergoing his second attempt at *The Trials*.
- **Axel:** A *Brond Helm* from the corner closest to the enemy.
- **Loa:** Daughter of Axel.
- **Red:** An ex-slave who escaped the howling pits of the *Stafntaki* and aspires to become a *Brond*.

The Ranks of the Brond

- **Brond Helm:** Keepers of the peace and judges of Northland.
- **Brond Voldur:** Honor guard and deputies of the *Brond Helm.*
- **Brond Here:** Bearers of the sword and protectors of the people.

The Men of the Mountains

- **Lady Strongbridge:** Ambassador of *Stor Doren*, the mountain under-kingdom, and conductor of *The Trials* during *The Gathering.*

The Enemy

- **Thane:** A formidable and ruthless leader known for his size, strength, and violent tactics.
- **Ambassador Egil:** The mouth of 'King' Thane.
- **The Stafntaki:** Thane's elite berserkers.

Mythic Characters

- **Rasmus:** The creator of this world that bears her name.
- **Fenreir:** An ancient wolf bound by chains, awaiting the end of the world.
- **Balder:** Keeper of the sky, bringer of the cold, giver of law, and guardian of the honored dead.
- **Freya:** Keeper of the ground, bringer of life and mercy.
- **The Vuloospa:** The first ones.

Places

- **Alstead:** The most prosperous city in Northland, known for trade and cultural exchange.
- **Stalden Keep:** The central stronghold located atop *Alstead.*
- **Stor Doren:** The fabled stronghold of the *Men of the Mountains.*
- **The Seven Corners:** Jurisdictions of the *Brond Helms* of Northland.

- **Stanheng Hol:** An ancient temple ringed with sandstone hedges where *Balder* inscribed the law—long ago.
- **Bálstaðr:** The burning place where fallen *Brond* are cremated.
- **Einsam Fjall:** The lonely mountain where *The Trials* begin.
- **Ey Sannhet:** The island of truth.
- **The Morass:** A deadly swamp where Thane has a fortress of his own.
- **Iz:** The ice moon where all Northlanders hope to travel after death.
- **Brond:** The fire moon, where the metal of the mountains falls from.
- **The Halls of Iz:** *Balder's* final resting place, where the brave live forever.
- **Great In-Between:** A mystical realm where past, present, and future converge.

ACKNOWLEDGMENTS

This book is the culmination of a decade-long journey exploring the nature of love, power, spirituality, and cruelty, all wrapped up in a mythological fable. To my wife, Michelle, thank you for your endless patience on every twist and turn during this process of discovery. To my family and friends, your support and insight has been a constant source of strength. This book would not exist without your belief in its potential.

To the talented artists of Ambient Pixel Design who brought this book's cover to life, inspired by the original concept art of Steve Wood and Brandon Rowe. Special thanks to Derek Walborn and Kacper Zwarzany, who helped me visualize the East Coast of Northland, and to Jesh Art Studio for crafting the chapter illustrations that enhance the atmosphere of this experience.

To Mayfly, and especially Julie Scheife, for being such incredible collaborators throughout this process. To my wonderful copyeditor, Candace Sinclair, for your sharp eye and invaluable perspective.

Finally, to the readers who embark on this journey with me, thank you for giving these characters and this world a place in your imagination.

Here's to the stories that find us—and to those we have yet to discover.

AUTHOR BIO

Sean is a storyteller at heart, crafting narratives across multiple mediums as both a writer and editor. A native of Baltimore, Sean now resides in Los Angeles, where he has built a dynamic career in film and television.

An eclectic geek, Sean is as likely to immerse himself in the intricacies of the Franco-Prussian War as he is to dissect the latest *Star Wars* trailer. With interests ranging from football to horror films, he brings a wealth of curiosity and creativity to his writing.

Sean's love for storytelling extends to the world of graphic novels, where his work has appeared in the anthology *321 Fast Comics*. These experiences, combined with his passion for mythmaking, inform his debut novel *Under the Horn of Hearth*.

www.ingramcontent.com/pod-product-compliance
Lightning Source LLC
Chambersburg PA
CBHW020148120726
47903CB00007B/2462